1-99

		DATE DUE	

SLEEPING WITH
PANCHO VILLA

SLEEPING

With

PANCHO VILLA

a novel by

RICK SKWIOT

University Press of Colorado

International Standard Book Number 0-87081-506-7

Published by the University Press of Colorado
P.O. Box 849
Niwot, Colorado 80544

The University Press of Colorado is a cooperative publishing enterprise
supported, in part, by Adams State College, Colorado State University,
Fort Lewis College, Mesa State College, Metropolitan State College of
Denver, University of Colorado, University of Northern Colorado,
University of Southern Colorado, and Western State College of Colo-
rado.

The paper used in this publication meets the minimum requirements of
the American National Standard for Information Sciences—Permanence
of Paper for Printed Library Materials. ANSI Z39.48-1984

Library of Congress Cataloging-in-Publication Data

Skwiot, Rick, 1947–
    Sleeping with Pancho Villa : a novel / by Rick Skwiot.
      p.   cm.
    ISBN 0-87081-506-7 (alk. paper)
    I. Title.
  PS3569.K89S59   1998
  813'.54—dc21   98-31024
                                                          CIP

07 06 05 04 03 02 01 00 99 98   10 9 8 7 6 5 4 3 2 1

For Veta

FOREWORD

Unlike those in most novels, the protagonist of this book is neither a man nor a woman but a village—a pueblito, to be exact—to whose will other, lesser characters must ultimately bend or break. As in other works of fiction, the characters and incidents in this panoramic novel are, by and large, imaginary.

SLEEPING WITH
PANCHO VILLA

Chapter

ONE

It was Friday afternoon, and Don Pablo Martínez sat sipping coffee and savoring his dessert, a piece of nut pie, at his regular table in the corner of the Café Cristóbal Colón. He sat thinking that what he liked best about the Revolutionary Party was that there was absolutely nothing revolutionary about it.

That made his nomination acceptance speech, which he was to give the next morning, a pleasant task. As Don Pablo took another bite of pie, he heard reverberating in his mind some of the key phrases he would use—phrases that he had honed and polished over years of making the same speech.

He would promise, if reelected party leader, to continue the policies that had worked so well over the past fifteen years to bring stability to the pueblito. Which was to say that he would name the same slate of men to be reelected mayor, chief of police, director of public works, and director of public revenue. Who would thus remain beholden to Don Pablo. Thus the stability.

None of this socialist nonsense for him or his town. Those Young Turks would have to wait their day. If there was one thing the Revolutionary Party would never tolerate, it was change.

He took another big bite of pie, heard a crack, and muttered aloud, "Ay, cabrón!" Except now when he spoke, he whistled, so it sounded to his ears as, "Sais, scabrónz!"

Don Pablo Martínez slipped the broken front tooth into his pocket and signaled closed-mouth to Jesús, the mesero, for his check.

Doctor Rafael Rodríguez took the dentures from Don Pablo and smiled.

"Sí, Don Pablo. There is no problem. First thing tomorrow morning. Seguro."

But he knew in his heart there was nothing sure about it and felt perspiration creep down his spine. A toothless and, Rodríguez thought, somehow less intimidating Don Pablo leaned across the big polished desk of his study toward the doctor, who stood before him.

"You must understand . . ." Here Don Pablo glanced to his left, then to his right, as though searching for a spy, but they were alone in the cavernous room. Doctor Rodríguez leaned closer as Don Pablo continued. "Subversive elements—within the Revolutionary Party!—plot to bring chaos to the municipality. As I represent order and prosperity, they will seize any opportunity to diminish me. They are like a pack of dogs. Any sign of weakness on my part and they will pounce."

The doctor nodded gravely, though understanding that Don Pablo spoke for effect and not without some hyperbole.

But to Don Pablo this was not exaggeration. He could imagine the impression he would make, for he had seen himself in the mirror: a feeble, toothless old man. Or, equally humiliating and precarious, a gap-toothed fool whistling words no one could take seriously. He could imagine the ridicule the Young Turks would spread. He could imagine them pouncing.

He stood, moved around the large desk, and gave Rodríguez an abrazo, the manly embrace that carried with it such a sense of obligation.

"I will not forget your service, Rodríguez. If not for friends like you, Rafael, where would a man like me be?"

Doctor Rafael Rodríguez sat in the corner of the Café Cristóbal Colón sipping a beer and staring at the gap-toothed dentures of Don Pablo Martínez resting on the table before him in a clear plastic bag.

He could not bring himself to accept Don Pablo's contention that subversive elements lurking within the Revolutionary Party were waiting to topple him from his position of power. Don Pablo was very powerful. It would never happen. Which meant he could not disappoint Don Pablo. To fail in this would be to lose the favor and patronage of Don Pablo. If that happened . . . Well, he did not want to think about the consequences.

But he did anyway: License difficulties. Misplaced tax payments. Endless foot-dragging on the building permit for the extra bedroom for his wife's mother. Accusations of malpractice. Problems with the police. It was apparent to Rodríguez that only Don Pablo stood between him and ruin. Which would not be a problem if he had a tooth with which to repair the denture of Señor Martínez.

To fix it in a week would not be a problem. He could order today from the catalog, and the tooth would arrive from the capital the following Friday.

To fix it by Tuesday would not be a big problem. He could take the Sunday bus to the capital, pick up the needed tooth at the dental supply house first thing Monday morning, and be back by Monday night.

But to fix it by tomorrow morning . . . He shook his head, sighed, and called to Jesús for another beer.

Jesús Balderas Banyón stood leaning against the jamb in the open doorway of the Café Cristóbal Colón, staring across the street at the red dress in the shop window of La Esmeralda.

He tried to picture Marielos in the dress. This was not a problem for Jesús, since he was an imaginative young man and since the mannequin who wore the dress had the same, slender figure as Marielos and no head, so he could simply place his wife's there in his fertile imagination. Yes, yes, he thought, and smiled his beautiful, even smile. Muy bella. They would be the handsomest couple in town.

But then his eyes dropped to a discarded gum wrapper in the gutter before him. For he had also seen the price of the dress, printed in large black numerals on a card attached to it at the waist. It cost more than a waiter made in a week—at least until the socialists bring justice, he told himself.

He could have saved for the dress, but he hadn't realized their anniversary was Saturday until Marielos happened to mention it, casually, at breakfast that morning. Their first anniversary. When she reminded him he acted as though he was pretending he had forgotten.

"Perhaps then we should go dancing tomorrow night," he said offhandedly.

She beamed but then, catching herself, shrugged and said, "But I have nothing to wear."

"Jesús. Jesús!"

He turned and saw Doctor Rodríguez in the corner, motioning for another beer.

The morning sun had barely peeked over the white stone wall into the garden, but Don Pablo Martínez was already pacing back and forth across the patio outside his dining room. He looked at his watch as he turned and saw that it was still ten minutes until Rodríguez was due.

The cook came out from the kitchen and asked, "Are you ready for breakfast, Señor Martínez?"

Tight-lipped, he shook his head. "No, no, Chucha. Not now."

She returned to the kitchen, and Don Pablo continued his pacing.

But soon Don Pablo heard a pounding on the outer door of his walled home and halted. Chucha scurried through the dining room and soon returned leading Doctor Rodríguez. In his hand he carried a clear plastic sack with Don Pablo's dentures inside.

After the doctor had fitted them in place, Don Pablo put his arm around Rodríguez's shoulder and squeezed, pulling the doctor to him.

"I will not forget this, Rodríguez. As a matter of fact, I will give my personal attention to your business license application. When it is due?"

Here it comes, Rodríguez thought. Don Pablo puts the bite on everyone.

"Soon," said the doctor, figuring that was something Don Pablo already knew.

"I can assure you, Rafael, that there will be no problem and no delay. I will see the mayor today. Now tell me, what is your charge for the denture?"

Doctor Rodríguez smiled a quivering, halfhearted smile as he remembered how much he had invested in repairing Don Pablo's denture.

"For you, Don Pablo, there is no charge."

As Don Pablo Martínez sat down to his breakfast of chilaquiles and took a lusty bite, on the other side of town Jesús Balderas Banyón gawked at his wife, Marielos, in her new red dress and whistled wolfishly through the gap in his row of beautiful white teeth. Then he kissed her passionately and left for the important Revolutionary Party meeting.

Meanwhile, Doctor Rafael Rodríguez walked over the rough, cobbled streets of his pueblito toward home and waiting patients, deciding that today—for one day only—he would charge double, in hopes of recouping his loss in fixing Don Pablo's denture.

Chapter

TWO

Jake sat sipping morning coffee in the Café Cristóbal Colón, reading in *Excelsior* how a nuclear reactor had melted down the previous day in Sinaloa, when Jordan came in, pulled up a chair, and said:

"I need some money."

Jake gave him twenty pesos.

Jordan said, "I'm keeping track of this. Double your money back when I sell some paintings."

Jake nodded and went back to his newspaper.

Jordan lived off a monthly check from the United States government, the Korean War having given him an ulcer, but he was always a month behind, or ahead, depending on how you looked at it. The money was usually gone within forty-eight hours of his cashing the check, to pay the previous month's creditors, and Jordan would then have to live by his wits until the next one came. However, he would go to Jake last, only after exhausting the other limited credit opportunities in town, the best of which were gringo tourists whom he would likely never see again. Jake, too, figured it as charity.

Jordan stared at the headline on Jake's newspaper.

"Are we upwind or downwind from Sinaloa?"

"Upwind." Jake made a sweeping motion with his arm from left to right. "Everything Mexican drifts up to the States."

"Great. That's all I'd need on top of everything else—radiation poisoning." Jordan was holding his stomach and grimacing.

"You'll feel better if you eat."

Jake hissed at the waiter, Jesús, and told him to put Mr. Freeman's breakfast on his bill. Jordan ordered, then turned to Jake.

"August 6, 1945."

Jake looked at him.

"Hiroshima," Jordan said.

"Before my time."

"I was in high school in Harlem. Next day my science teacher, Mr. Van Uven, tells us: 'Class, open your texts to page one twenty-five. There you'll find the sentence, "The atom is the basic, irreducible unit of matter." Take up your pens, class, and cross out that sentence.' "

It was a good story, but Jake wondered what Jordan was doing in school in the middle of summer. Perhaps he had gone to summer school. Or maybe his memory was foggy, and it truly happened a month later, after Labor Day, when the fall semester began. Also, Jordan was an artist, therefore creative, and some of his stories where just too good to be entirely true. But this was a good story and believable, so Jake didn't question the schism in dates.

"The world respected us in those days," Jordan said. "I went to Tokyo on R and R in the spring of fifty-three, and the Japanese girls kissed me and called me 'Atomic G.I.' "

"Not respect, fear. Everyone was scared shitless of Armageddon."

"Same-same."

Jordan's eggs with jalapeños arrived, and Jake went on while Jordan ate:

"I started school in sixty-two. On the first day a siren goes off, and the teacher tells us to crouch beneath our desks and cover our heads. I recall peeking out the window for the mushroom cloud. That's how my formal education began: learning the correct posture for oblivion. Then every time a plane flew over I'd look up and await the Bomb. In the middle of Illinois, for Christ's sake."

As he was speaking, Jake became conscious of a voice over his shoulder.

"Se venden puercos que . . ."

He turned and saw a small, brown-skinned girl holding a hand-carved pig.

"No, no, gracias. No lo quiero," Jake said and turned back to Jordan to continue his story.

But the girl repeated, "Pigs for sale . . ." and went on with her sales pitch in a singsong voice. She had it memorized and, once she got it going, apparently couldn't turn it off.

Jordan took the pig from the girl and leaned toward her barely audible voice. Then he removed a small cork that served as the wooden pig's snout and gazed inside.

"Did you hear what she said? The pig's hollow, and you put houseflies inside. They buzz around bumping pegs that make its ears and tail move."

Jake looked from the pig to the girl. She was round-faced,

with large, chocolate eyes and a finger in her mouth.

"From the folks who brought you the Spanish Inquisition."

"We've got to try this."

Jake gave the girl five pesos for the pig and watched her go off carrying her plastic sack filled with housefly torture chambers.

"Now," said Jordan, "all we need are some flies."

Jake motioned toward Jesús. The waiter came over, and Jordan showed him the pig and how it worked.

"Now all we need are some flies," Jordan reiterated in Spanish.

"Vivas?"

"Of course. If they are to fly they must be alive."

"Of course. Let's go look in the kitchen."

Jordan went off with Jesús while Jake sat staring at the pig, thinking how varied his life had become in Mexico.

Within minutes Jordan returned holding a napkin over a paper cup, Jesús following close behind.

They agreed that errant flies would, in principle, more likely seek altitude than dive, so Jordan held the pig nose down and fed flies vertically up its snout. He got three in and lost a fourth before managing to replace the cork. Then he set the pig on the table, and the three men gathered round it like scientists encircling an experiment.

They leaned closer, heard a faint humming coming from the beast, then saw the ears wiggle. The curled plastic tail of the pig wagged, and its white, dotted eyes began crossing and rolling. Simultaneously the three men broke into peals of laughter.

Jordan threw back his head and bellowed deeply, holding his sides; tears rolled down Jesús's cheeks; and Jake shook with delight, the three of them reveling in their mischief like a tri-

umvirate of malevolent gods, gods who had created an eter-
nally amusing hell for their blind charges, who buzzed about
aimlessly, pointlessly, in the dark.

"Todas las gringas son putas," Marcos said, showing Don Pablo his new watch. "This one had a husband in Houston—a lawyer—who permits his whore of a wife to travel alone. Yes, they are all whores, the bitches from the United States."

Don Pablo Martínez sipped his coffee. "Truly. Not like Mexican maidens. And did she . . ."

Don Pablo looked about the Café Cristóbal Colón. At this time of morning only men sat at the tables, the businessmen and property owners he had known his whole life. Still, Don Pablo gestured economically, delicately pointing a finger toward his mouth.

"Did she . . .?"

Marcos leaned forward, and the silver medal of San Martín de Porres, the patron saint of artists and drunkards, swung out of his unbuttoned white shirt on a thick silver chain, dangling on the oilcloth tabletop.

"Constantly. Even on the bus. And at night, in the hotel room, I would wake to find her there." For effect, Marcos whispered, letting his eyes drop for an instant as though watching her there.

Don Pablo sucked his teeth. "Híjole! What a whore!" And he signaled to the waiter.

When Jesús came over, Don Pablo laid a hand on Marcos's shoulder. "I wish to invite you for a drink, hijo."

"Gracias, Don Pablo." Then to Jesús: "Cerveza, por favor." Even though it was barely nine a.m., a beer was what he needed. Marcos explained to Don Pablo:

"That crazy gringa had me awake all night, drinking Cuba libres and tearing up my bed. And as I put her on the bus for the border this morning, she kissed me and put her hand there. Qué puta!"

Don Pablo laughed and clapped him on the back. "Well, drink up, Marcos, then get some rest. Another bus returns from the border tonight."

Marcos Celorio Villareal stood stripped to the waist on the terrace of his casita, bending to the left ten times with the iron weight held behind his head, then to the right ten times. Next he lay flat on the palm mat with the weight still held behind his head and began doing sit-ups.

Each time he rose, Marcos saw a blue sky, majestic black mountains, a distant green valley. Inside the white walls that ringed his home, he saw a purple jacaranda tree, pulsing crimson bougainvillea, and a shining green palm growing in the garden below.

It was a modest house, but one his visitors found "charming." Two stories, an enclosed red-brick patio, and startlingly beautiful sunsets, when white egrets would return to their nests atop tall firs at the bottom of the hill. The pale women from Toronto, Minneapolis, and New Jersey loved the sunsets and the flowers and enjoyed sunbathing half naked on the patio. They loved, too, Marcos's bronze body, his hard stomach, and tight buttocks. But the house was his great good fortune—though he had earned it.

He had been young then, very young, and she not so very young and not so young as she pretended. He laughed to himself again at her belief that she was supporting and encouraging an aspiring young artist. When she finally figured it out, she stopped coming to Mexico, and the checks stopped coming, too. But by then he had the house. She had put it in his name as a formality, since foreigners could not own property directly in Mexico. But once she realized the score, she never again showed her face in town and never contested ownership of the house. Now fifteen years had passed, and she could very well be dead, he thought.

The warm sun cutting through the thin mountain air felt good on his chest. He took just enough sun to keep his skin bronze yet not so much as to make it brown. Just as he grew his hair long enough to look somewhat Indian but not so long as not to look prosperous. Most other mestizos—that is, most Mexicans—saw their Indian blood as an embarrassment or even a handicap to social success. But not Marcos. The blonde gringas came to Mexico for something dark, exotic, and different—but not too different. And that was what he gave them.

He could feel cool perspiration on his body as it dispelled the past night's rum and the beer he'd drunk that morning with Don Pablo. Soon he would take his siesta. Then soon again it would be night.

He knew she would be the one. As Marcos crossed the patio of the crowded restaurant, he saw how she looked at him: boldly and with curiosity. She was with two others neither as striking nor as bold as she, and as Marcos greeted the patrona, Doña Cristina, with a kiss upon the cheek, he noticed beneath the bold one's auburn hair how the blue eyes remained trained on him.

Perhaps the auburn was not her own color. Many times he had taken blonde gringas to bed only to discover they were not true rubias. But this one had the pale eyes, so maybe it was true. And with this one he would need no introduction, no ruse. To be as direct as she was would serve best. Besides, these were not Mexican women. You could do with them as you liked without fear.

When the guitar player finished his song, Marcos simply walked back across the patio of the open-air restaurant to their table and introduced himself. There was no need to be clever, only charming, and his English was plenty good for that.

"Good evening. A lovely night. Hope you are enjoying our pueblito. I have not seen your faces before—I would have remembered. When did you arrive?"

Usually some combination of those pleasantries was sufficient, and it was this time as well. The musician began another Andalusian tune on his guitar, and, begging permission, Marcos slid into the vacant chair at the table as though allowing the other diners a better view of the entertainment.

He shook hands around the table and remembered all their names. The other two wished to talk, but the auburn-haired one—her name was Stacy—said little. But she was not cold or indifferent. He knew she wanted him.

"There is little entertainment in our town," he told them after the plain ones confirmed they had just arrived. "But the sunsets are lovely, and the weather is always spring, and many North Americans come for a week and stay for years to enjoy the peace and solitude."

The plain ones were easily charmed, he could see, but Stacy looked at him with a slight smile and eyes that seemed to see through the charming mask. The other two asked the inevitable questions asked by women unaccustomed to and uninterested in peace and solitude. He answered:

"Yes, there is one place, not far away, with music and dancing, a very respectable place where I would be honored to escort you."

Hardly anyone ever said no.

He danced with them all and invested in a round of drinks, but after that, as usual, his money was no good. For gringas, the women danced nicely to the Latin music, their loose skirts flowing in the night air. They did not jump around like fools as some did after a few margaritas, but moved with restraint and grace. Their clothes did not at first strike him as expensive but felt so when he danced with the women. And the perfume of the red-haired one seemed richer and more subtle than any he had known.

He held her close as they danced and said, "How long will you stay in our town?"

She shrugged. "As long as I enjoy myself."

He smiled. "I offer my services."

"Which include?"

"Lo que quieres. Whatever you wish."

"I wish a man," she said and looked him straight in the eye.

He was right. This gringa was a bold one.

Marcos again pressed the barbell over his head and looked down from the terrace adjoining his bedroom to the walled patio below. There Stacy basked naked in the morning sun— yet somehow revealed nothing.

This one is different, he thought. Even though they had slept together for a week now and had made love a dozen times, and even though he was a man of the world and she was just twenty-four, he could not get under her skin as he had with all the others. Yes, she would do whatever he asked in bed and even some things he would not not have suspected of such a beautiful woman, even if she was a gringa. Yet once that had ended, there was the mask again that kept him from feeling as though he had penetrated her. In fact, at times it almost felt as if she had penetrated him, and before her eyes, for the first time as a man, he felt self-conscious about his nakedness.

Marcos replaced the barbell on the palm frond mat and moved through the open doors to the bedroom. There he grabbed a towel that he hung around his neck and descended to the patio.

Stacy lay on a towel in the sun. She lay on her back with her head on a pillow, sunglasses on her nose, but otherwise naked. In her hand was a thick book by Leo Tolstoy, and he wondered what she got from such things. Her pubic hair was not auburn but light brown, and she tanned well for a gringa with blue eyes.

She heard him approach and soon looked up to him standing above her. She smiled. Marcos said:

"I was going to the kitchen to make juice. I could bring you some."

"First come here and make love to me," she commanded.

Marcos looked around as though inspecting for a possible audience. "Here?"

She laid the book down and reached up to tug at his zipper. "Fuck me now, here on the hard stones."

Marcos smiled and slid his legs from his white jeans, standing above her with his penis thickening. He assumed the arrogant posture of an Aztec warrior over a conquered maiden. She feigned fright, falling back onto the towel and cowering, but he knew, as she did, that they were play-acting and in fact it was he who was being ravished.

Don Pablo Martínez rose from his comida at his corner table of the Café Cristóbal Colón, shook Marcos's hand, and bowed from the waist toward Stacy. They moved past Don Pablo to take a table by the window as Jesús scurried up to pull out her chair.

Marcos liked taking Stacy to the Café Cristóbal Colón, or to any public place. It had been nearly a month now that they had been together, and he never tired of it. She was the sort of woman whose presence on a man's arm invested him with status. Now even Don Pablo treated Marcos with deference, where before he had been pleasant yet paternal.

Stacy was both beautiful and elegant, and Marcos thought with horror of his shame should she ever discover what sort of gringas had preceded her in his bed, what sort of whores he had proudly escorted about town. Loud women in garish makeup, women old enough to be his mother . . . He didn't want to think about it. That life was gone, and a new, beautiful, and admirable existence lay before him.

She reached across the table to take his hand and held it on top of the menu.

"Marcos, I have to go away for a few days. I got a letter today from Father. Family business. I'll take the morning bus."

He looked at her thinking that perhaps he should offer to go with her. Meeting her father would be a good thing now that they had talked about being together always. But as though reading his mind, she added:

"You can come next time. Grandmother is ill. Now is not good."

"I am sorry about your grandmother," he said.

But he really wasn't. He was sorry about being excluded, even temporarily, from her family.

"When I return we will be together."

"Siempre," he added.

She smiled and squeezed his hand. "Yes. Always."

A few days later Don Pablo asked about her.

"Where is your beautiful lady, Marcos? I have not seen her."

"There is an illness in the family. She had to return to Texas for a time."

"Don't let that one get away, hijo."

"No. She may return tomorrow."

But she didn't. Nor the next day. After a week Marcos went to the long-distance office and placed a call to her number in Austin. A woman with a Mexican accent answered the telephone and went to get Stacy for him.

"Marcos! How good to hear your voice."

He asked about her and about her grandmother.

"She's the same, I'm afraid. She may go at any time. As a matter of fact, we were just leaving for the hospital."

"Te quiero," he said. "I love you."

He had said that before to other women, but this time it

hurt when he said it. Love had meant only pleasure to Marcos. Now he saw there was an element of pain to it as well.

"You, too," she said. "Have to go. I'll write."

The line went dead, and Marcos felt something bad inside. She did not sound like the same woman he had made love to. Yes, it was she, but something was different. And "I'll write." It sounded like she wasn't coming back right away.

He put down the receiver and paid the young woman operator for the call.

A few days later Marcos decided to write Stacy a letter, a brief letter. His spoken English was fine—the gringas had been good for that—but writing was another thing.

He dusted off the typewriter that the first one, the old woman who gave him the house, had left behind, and found some typing paper in the desk. Using his index fingers, he typed:

Dear Stacy,

Hello! Hope Grandmother is well. I think of me and you making love in the sun. See you soon!

Love,
Marcos

On a yellowed envelope that he found in a tray beneath the typewriter, Marcos typed her address in Austin, Texas, USA, and carried the letter to the post office.

Mail between the two countries traveled slowly. He knew he would get no reply for at least a week, maybe two. But a third week passed without any communication, then a fourth.

Marcos never knew time could be such an enemy. Each day seemed never-ending. He had no interest in going to the bars to see what had come into town, no interest in drinking or dancing. He was interested only in Stacy's return.

Marcos avoided the Café Cristóbal Colón, for every time he went in, Don Pablo would ask about her. And without Stacy at his side, Don Pablo treated Marcos as he had before, as a son, a boy. Until he had met Stacy, he had never really noticed it, so it never bothered him. Now it did.

One day Marcos again went to the long-distance office and gave the operator the number. When the connection was made, she nodded toward a booth against the wall.

Again the woman with the Mexican accent answered, and Marcos spoke to her in Spanish, asking to talk to Stacy.

"La señorita no está a casa."

"When will she return?"

"No sé. She left yesterday. I do not know when she will return."

Marcos thanked her and rang off.

It was the first good news he'd had in a month. She was on her way. Any day now she would appear.

But three days passed, and a fourth, then a week, and he was still alone. Then on the eighth day it came.

Marcos had continued his daily regimen: exercise, fresh fruit, brisk walks in the surrounding campo. If anything, he was more diligent than ever, at times exercising twice a day, and his long, solitary walks becoming even longer and somehow more solitary. On this particular morning, as he was bending and stretching on the roof, he heard the metal cover of the mail slot in the front door creak open and drop back with a clang, and he knew it was a letter from Stacy. His intuitions were almost always right.

Marcos disciplined himself against running downstairs for the letter. Rather, he would finish his workout as always, squeeze oranges in the downstairs kitchen for his juice, then retrieve the letter.

When he had done his sit-ups and sweat glistened on his tanned, washboard stomach muscles, he stepped to the bedroom, grabbed a towel, and sauntered down the steps to the patio in a delicious cloud of anticipation.

In the kitchen at the rear of the casita, he squeezed oranges and poured the juice into a tall, thick glass that he then carried to the front sala facing the street. There, lying on the stone floor beneath the mail slot, was a letter with the tiny, red–white–and–blue stamp of the gringo flag. He bent for it, saw the Austin postmark, and slipped it into the waistband of his sweatpants. Marcos wanted to savor this moment, to make it fill his dry, desertlike day. He wanted to enjoy again the feeling that a beautiful new life awaited him.

Upstairs, he carried a sling chair from his bedroom to the adjoining terrace, lowered himself into it, and set the glass of bright yellow juice on the stone floor. Marcos pulled the dampened envelope from where it was held against his perspiring body and frowned at it.

He hadn't noticed when he first picked it up that the envelope was very light and thin. A short letter.

He held it up to the sun, and what he saw made hot blood rush to his face. Marcos tore open the envelope, yanked out the solitary piece of paper, and sat staring at it.

After a moment he looked up to the sun with tortured face, like a wounded Aztec warrior beseeching Quetzalcoatl for justice, then back down to the paper in his hand.

He studied the signature, read the name of the Texas bank, and saw how much she thought he was worth, how much she

valued the services he had offered her. Then he wadded the
check in his fist and cast it to the garden below. It fell where she
had lain naked on the stones, and he saw himself being sum-
moned to her and obeying, saw what he had been.

Marcos rose from the sling chair, grabbed it by the metal
armrests, and yelled a dark, piercing scream, like that of a beast
whose flesh had just been penetrated by an arrow. He pitched
the chair from the terrace, and it clanged to the stones below,
where the memory of her lay.

Then, through the open doors of the bedroom, he spied
the bed where he had slept with her, where he had serviced her
night and day. He rushed in and tore the mattress from the bed,
then ran tugging it behind him to the terrace and jettisoned it
below.

On the desk by the window he saw the typewriter that had
produced the letter he sent her. God, how she must have laughed!
Did she show her friends the scratchings of the primitive? Did
she describe to her two girlfriends the hardness of his body and
the ready firmness of his prick, how eager and obedient he was?
Marcos grabbed the typewriter by the carriage as though grab-
bing the hair of the old woman who had left it and in whose
house he lived, and flung it from the terrace to the hard stones
below, where it landed with a crunch, breaking in two.

Marcos ripped the gold watch from his wrist, and that, too,
went down. Then the pictures from the bedroom wall: the framed
photographs of Marcos and Stacy, his pen-and-ink self-portrait,
his watercolor of the patio, the glass breaking on the stones, and
all lay in the garden like trash, as though a garbage truck had
come and despoiled Eden.

Marcos collapsed to the terrace floor, sitting abruptly on
the petate de palma where he did his daily exercises, and stared
out over the roofs of his town. Someone pounded on the down-

stairs door, and a neighbor called out over the wall:

"Marcos! Qué pasa, Marcos? Estás bien?"

But Marcos did not hear. He sat and stared out over the rooftops to the magnificent green valley in the distance and the majestic mountains and the clear blue sky—at the totality of the charming view that his hard-earned home afforded.

Chapter

FOUR

He had just started across the zócalo, moving under the elms with white-painted trunks, where boat-tailed grackles were screeching noisily and settling in for the night, when he heard a voice calling through the din of the birds:

"Amigo . . . Amigo . . ."

Then another:

"Hey, Jake!"

A green-and-white cab circling the town square counter-clockwise pulled up to the curb on the other side of a low wall. Guillermo was at the wheel, looking wan and translucent, and beside him in the front seat was Jordan. Jake stepped over the wall to shake Guillermo's cool, limpid hand and squatted down to peer across to Jordan, who said:

"We've got problems, man. Get in."

Jake slid into the back seat, and Jordan handed him a fifth of tequila—the cheapest sort, Jake saw, which came in a clear bottle that looked like glass until you picked it up and squeezed it and realized it was plastic. He took a pull from the bottle and handed it up to Guillermo, who gazed at him in the mirror with woeful eyes, and Jake feared the worst. Guillermo was dying, and the local doctors were doing their best, but that wasn't enough. What he needed was to get to Mexico City or some place where there was a real hospital. Jake could tell from his skin, the way it almost glowed, that he didn't have long to go. A wife and four kids, too.

But that wasn't it at all. As Guillermo moved the taxi from the curb, Jordan turned to Jake, took a slug from the bottle, and wiped his mouth with the back of his hand.

"The landlord, Don Pablo, needs my place. His niece is getting married, and he wants to set up house for them there."

"What about the mural?"

Jordan stared at him, and Jake saw a scared look in his eye. "We've got problems, man."

Guillermo locked the cab as Jordan opened the thick, old wooden door to his home, and they followed him through it into the patio. The sun had just set, and the vine-choked patio looked like a jungle. Guillermo and Jake waited just inside the door until Jordan had picked his way through the foliage and turned on lights under the veranda. Then they too moved forward through the jungle, and as they did the Mural of Fear became visible to them behind the columns of the veranda. They stopped before it, and Jordan brought chairs for them from inside.

Jake sat, lit a cigarette, and studied the mural. It was a good, yet stupid, work of art by a man who lived off a government check barely adequate even for Mexico, a hungry artist who needed to sell some canvases. But he spent his time painting a twenty-foot-long mural on the wall of a rented house. The mural appeared to consume him, like some seemingly benign but ultimately voracious cancer.

Jordan picked limes from a tree in the patio and passed them to his two guests along with the plastic tequila bottle. Guillermo and Jake drank and bit into the limes.

"Quién es este?" Guillermo asked, gesturing with the bottle toward a figure of a man.

"Es Mao Zedong," Jordan explained, "el jefe comunista de China y la Revolución de Cultura. For gringos, the communists are evil spirits, like the devil."

"Y estos?"

"Those are sinners being fed to the fires of Hell, the flames of eternal damnation that puritans fear."

Jordan began pointing out to the cabbie other elements in the mural that manifested American fear: Negroes, terrorists, and foreign hordes; serpents, darkness, disease.

Guillermo shook his head. "Gringos are fools to fear such things. It only invites death."

Jake caught Jordan's eye, but neither said a thing.

Fodder for the mural came in part from American newspapers and magazines, which Jordan read whenever he could find them, since he himself hadn't been back to the States for twenty-five years—a seeming manifestation of his own fears. But the best aspects of the mural, Jake thought, came not from *Time* or *Newsweek* but from deep inside Jordan. Such as his father, a stern, menacing presence looming over the left half of the mural like a wrathful black God. Beneath him a scroll with Gothic lettering read: "My eye is on you, boy." Or the trio of comely yet malevolent witches at the bottom right who stirred a living, yonic cauldron filled with mementos of childhood: toys, kittens, and Mother Goose.

Yet at the center of the mural was bare white wall. That was the part Jordan couldn't seem to finish, the one unifying element that would hold it all together.

"When does Don Pablo want the house?" Jake asked.

"By next month. His niece won't be married till fall, but the workers need time to repair the garden and to plaster and paint." Jordan looked at his mural. "The sons of bitches will come in with rollers." He took a drink of tequila, pulled a lime from the tree behind him, and bit into it. "Why now, after all these years? And just when I'm about to finish it."

Jake looked at Jordan and saw that it was just wishful thinking. He still had no idea what went in the center.

"Do you know this niece of Don Pablo?"

Jordan shook his head and asked Guillermo. Guillermo said, "I know who she is."

"Does she look like Don Pablo?"

"No. She is young and beautiful and could marry anyone."

"And what about her fiancé?"

"An asshole called Pancho."

"That narrows it," Jake said.

"He is a mere asshole of a sculptor," said Guillermo. "Not a true artist like you, Jordan."

"Tamayo, Orozco, Siqueiros, Rivera," Jordan said, holding up four fingers. "The four great Mexican revolutionary painters, and"—he stuck up his thumb—"I'm number five. I'm going to finish the revolution."

Jordan saw Guillermo staring at him intently and realized he had lapsed into English. "Do you know these men, the greatest of your artists?" he asked in Spanish.

Guillermo shook his head.

"Orozco's fresco at Guadalajara is the agnostic answer to Michelangelo's Sistine Chapel."

Guillermo again shook his head. Jordan explained:

"Many years ago, on the ceiling of the pope's chapel at the Vatican, Michelangelo painted a fresco of the Creation. In it God reaches out to touch Adam's fingertip, investing man with life and establishing the relationship between God and man."

As he spoke, Jordan stretched out his arm, first as an all-powerful yet benevolent Creator, then, turning around and assuming a meek and innocent demeanor, as Adam.

"Then, at Guadalajara," Jordan went on, "Orozco created a similar painting on the ceiling of the rotunda of El Hospicio Cabañas. But instead of God and Adam touching, two men reach out for one another—but never touch. They are forever frozen in a godless solitude." And Jordan stood at the center of his mural, caught in the bright spotlights he'd arranged so he could work on the wall both night and day, his long, dark fingers outstretched, grasping at air, a look of existential pain on his smooth, mahogany face.

"And in the capital, at the Fine Arts Palace, is Rivera's *Man in the Time Machine.* Not the original. *That* the Rockefellers destroyed out of fear. This is Rivera's replica."

Taking on a cowlike look of stupidity, Jordan told of the blond gringo astronaut in the center of the mural at the controls of the time machine. Then he emulated Lenin, Trotsky, and the enraged workers on the right half of the mural and the symbols of capitalism and repression on the left: the indifferent sophisticates sipping champagne, the mesmerized middle class, the gas-masked armies and looming bombers, Jordan diving fiercely at Guillermo, arms spread as wings. He described, too, the forces of nature—ice and fire, the heavens and earth, the flora and amoebic fauna—over which the time machine was superimposed.

Jordan went over to Jake for more tequila, and Guillermo

stared fixedly at the white space in the center of the mural as though he saw Rivera's masterpiece reflected there.

"God must allow you to finish your work," Guillermo suddenly said. "Your picture must be preserved."

Jordan handed him the tequila bottle. Guillermo took a swig and went on:

"There are three things a man must do before he dies: plant a tree, father a child, and write a book. In this picture, Jordan, you have done all three. It is your seed, your child, your story."

Jake glanced at Jordan and saw him looking back, thinking the same thing: Guillermo was a goner. He talked like a dead man.

Jordan asked him, "When did you last see the doctor?"

The Mexican shrugged. "Yesterday."

"And what did he do?"

"He examined me here and gave me some medicine."

Guillermo lifted up his shirt and pressed the area just below the armpit. He had cancer of the lymph glands and had gone for help too late, and the help he got was not so good.

"What did the doctor say?"

"He said to rest and to stay away from the curandera."

"Why would he say that?"

"Only because he is afraid she might cure me and then the town find out, and he would be out of business as a doctor."

"So you went to her."

"Sí."

"What did the witch do?"

"She chased the evil spirits into an egg and spilled the blood of a rooster and gave me this to take."

He took a vial from his shirt pocket and passed it to Jake. Jake pulled out the stopper and sniffed.

"Turpentine," he said, and handed it to Jordan.

"What did she say to do with this?"

"To put a spoonful in water and drink it three times a day. It is tonic."

"It is turpentine," Jake told him in Spanish. "Poison."

Jordan poured out a bit on the stone floor and lit it. It burned a short, blue-green flame. Then he got a bottle from the table where his paints and brushes lay and carried it to Guillermo.

"Smell. Now this. It's the same. Turpentine. I use it to clean paintbrushes. Don't drink this shit, hombre."

Guillermo nodded obediently, but Jake could tell he was going to take it anyway. It was all he had.

Jordan made a torch out of an old paintbrush doused with Guillermo's turpentine, and they all lit cigarettes off it. Then they passed around the tequila and stared quietly at the Mural of Fear.

After a silent minute—silent except for the noise of crickets in the jungle behind them—a shape suddenly appeared at the center of the mural, a small, dark shape moving across the bare white wall.

Guillermo stood, strode to the mural, and plucked a scorpion off the wall with his fingers. Then he dropped it to the stone floor and crushed it beneath his boot.

"Asshole of an alacrán," he said and sat down with a look of satisfaction.

For the next few weeks Jake saw very little of Jordan and nothing of Guillermo. Jordan did not drop by the Café Cristóbal Colón mornings to mooch breakfast as he often did, since his landlord, Don Pablo Martínez, was always there at his corner table, drinking coffee and cutting deals. Similarly, Jordan was not answering the door for fear it might be Don Pablo with his strong-arm men to put him on the street. But after three weeks Jordan showed up at Jake's place.

Jake rented a small room on the roof of an old colonial house and was in his hammock on the terrace taking the sun when he heard a knock at the door. Below he saw the maid moving from her washing to answer it, and soon Jordan was coming up the concrete stairs to the terrace. He spread his arms like a crucifix and proclaimed:

"I am saved! Resurrected!"

Jake looked at him from the hammock and waited for an explanation.

"I saw Don Pablo in the street. He no longer needs the house. He says it's mine as long as I want it. Híjole!"

Jordan began shadowboxing, ready to take on the world.

"What made him change his mind?"

Jordan clapped his hands and did a dance.

"The fiancé died!"

Jake later realized he should have asked then how the fiancé of Don Pablo's niece had died, but it didn't occur to him at the time. People were always dying in Mexico. All he knew was that by the grace of God, Jordan's mural had been spared.

But Guillermo soon followed the fiancé to the grave, and his death seemed to affect Jordan strangely. He sprang for a big spray of flowers for the casket and afterward did whatever he could to help Guillermo's widow and children. And whenever Jake met him on the street he seemed agitated.

"I'm working, man. Catch me later."

That was all he would say.

Most odd was the day Jake saw Jordan going into the cathedral. He followed him in and found Jordan, an avowed atheist, kneeling in the front pew with hands folded, as though praying. Jake stepped back behind a thick stone column and watched. After a minute Jordan crossed himself and rose, then moved to a small altar on the right side of the church where he lit a red votive candle and dropped a coin in the poor box.

Jake slipped out without being seen but couldn't figure it. Perhaps Jordan had made some sort of promise to Guillermo, he reasoned.

Then, one afternoon the following week, the maid brought an envelope upstairs to Jake. His name was written on the outside in an elegant hand, and beneath it was a black thumbprint. Inside he found a note from Jordan:

"Come tonight at eight."

It was nearly eight-thirty by the time Jake arrived at Jordan's house and found that the outer door had been left ajar. Sounds of music and conversation poured through it into the street.

He slid through the door into the patio and saw perhaps two dozen people under the veranda—some dancing to a mariachi band in the corner, others chatting and drinking, and still others admiring the Mural of Fear.

As Jake emerged from the junglelike patio, Jordan spied him and waved him over to a makeshift bar he had set up on his work table. He poured a brandy for Jake, who asked:

"What's the occasion?"

"The mural—it's finished."

"Then you found what you needed for the center?"

Jordan did not answer but put his arm around Jake's shoulder and led him toward the wall:

"Perdón. Permítame, por favor."

The crowd parted for them, and as they stood before the

completed mural, Jake felt a sudden coldness, as though glimpsing some dark and secret ritual. For enwombed at the center of the mural sat Guillermo with his pale, translucent skin, curled like a mustached fetus in a black egg of death, and on his face the certain knowledge of that death, a horrible awareness of its coming. He sat cut off from the surrounding jungle of fear, besieged, alone in his fortress, forever waiting.

Jake turned to Jordan, and their eyes met, and Jake knew that Guillermo had done it, that he had killed the future husband of Don Pablo's niece. Jordan shook his head and whispered:

"I knew nothing about it, Jake. It was a gift."

Chapter

FIVE

The old woman and the dead man came in as Jake and Jordan were trying to explain to the owner how to make gringo shrimp sauce. But neither of them could think of the Mexican word for horseradish, perhaps because they were both fairly drunk, though it was only the afternoon.

"Es una salsa blanca y bien picante," Jordan said to the owner, "de una legumbre que se llama en inglés 'horseradish.'"

The owner of the restaurant, a young and accommodating Veracruzano, who had recently opened the place, shook his head and shrugged.

"I will add picante sauce," he said in Spanish, "and it will be the same."

"No, it is not the same," Jake said. "You must have gringo cocktail sauce if you want the gringos to come in for your seafood. You must have 'horseradish.'" He pointed to his shrimp cocktail. "This sauce is like dessert. It is too sweet for gringos."

"Yo uso solamente limón y catsup," said the owner, except that when he pronounced the last word in Spanish it sounded like "cat soup."

"Ah, este es el problema," said Jordan. "La cat soup mexicana es muy dulce." He turned to Jake. "The cat soup is too sweet."

"Muy dulce. Too damn dulce." Jake drained off the beer from the bottom of his bottle. "Another?"

"You go ahead. I'll wait."

Jake signaled to the owner's wife, who was tending the bar, which was no more than a laminated countertop with a used refrigerator behind it, where they kept lukewarm beer and refrescos.

"Otra, por favor."

"Dos?"

"Una."

She pulled a Victoria from the refrigerator, opened it, and strutted over to their folding metal card table, which was covered with an oilcloth. They sat on folding metal chairs. The restaurant, like most things in town, was undercapitalized.

As she approached the two men, their eyes strayed to where her tight jeans ran up her crevice in front and—after she set the beer on the card table, leered at Jake, and turned to walk away—where they ran up her crevice in back.

Since the first round they had been ordering one beer at a time—first Jake, then Jordan, then Jake, then Jordan—and each time she'd walk over in her tight jeans and give one or both of them a sultry glance. Jake found her promenades only mildly diverting, but it was a small town where there rarely was any true entertainment. More entertaining, though, was that her accommodating husband pretended not to notice any of it and actually made a point of looking away when they ogled his wife.

It was somewhere during the horseradish conversation and ritualized beer delivery that the old American couple came in from the sunshine through the open door.

Jake first noticed the old man: head hanging to one side, jaw slack; a slow, shuffling gait aided by a cane; eyes that seemed to gaze fearfully at something inside his own head. The old woman was more or less normal.

They walked to the table at the back. There were only three tables, and they left the center one empty. When they had passed, Jordan whispered:

"Stroke."

"Something got him," Jake said. "He's all fouled up."

But once the couple took the table at the back, Jake and Jordan forgot about them and got back to pondering the Spanish word for horseradish and ordering solitary beers.

Half an hour later, after they had given up on horseradish and were talking about the owner's refusing to acknowledge his wife's flirtations, and about marriage in Mexico and tight jeans in general, they heard coming from the back table:

"You're not contributing. You've got to contribute. Look at you. You just sit there with that face."

It was the old woman laying into him. Jake and Jordan sat silent and listened.

"Look at that face. And with your mouth open. You're not contributing. I'm doing my part, I'm holding up my end. I'm making conversation and exchanging information, but I get no input from you. Where's *your* input?"

The old man showed no reaction at all to her line of questioning, gave no input whatsoever, contributed nothing. To keep the conversation going she said:

"How do you think I feel, looking at that face all through my meal? Do you ever consider anyone but yourself? Do you ever think how I might feel?"

Jordan sneered and muttered to Jake out the right side of his mouth, showing his gold tooth: "I'm gonna whip her ass for the old guy. Brotherhood, man. We need to stick together."

Jake took a pull from his bottle. "She really ought to cut him some slack. She's giving him no slack whatsoever."

Jordan stared at the old woman, and his eyes got even glassier. "Watch me, man. I'm gonna do something niggerish."

Jake winced, not out of any delicacy about Jordan's language but because he knew what it meant. Jordan had a way of being confrontational at times with white folks, including Jake. Jake thought it was his growing up in Harlem that made him so aggressive—and maybe that the war had messed him up. Whatever the underlying causes, occasionally Jordan would boil over at a relatively minor thing, threatening and insulting whoever he believed had crossed him and gesticulating so wildly that Jake thought he would start a brawl. Usually nothing came of it, but it still bothered the hell out of Jake—offended his "Caucasian propriety," Jordan would say, making it sound like an incurable and shameful disease. Jordan was certainly not confined by it. But Jake knew that if he cautioned him now, Jordan would feel shackled and thus honor-bound to act as niggerish as he could, so he remained silent.

The old woman felt Jordan staring at her or heard them talking low, for she turned and fixed Jordan with a gaze, and his eyes locked onto hers, and all was suddenly quiet. Jake saw Jordan move as though to speak and said to himself, "Here he goes." But then he heard the old woman say:

"Are you from New York?"

Jordan hesitated an instant then seemed to soften.

"I was raised there," he said.

"I heard you talking and thought you were from New York.

Boston. We're from Boston. We live near Harvard."

"Are you a teacher?" Jordan asked.

"Used to be. Secondary school. Mathematics."

"That explains it," Jake said.

"What? Explains what?"

"Your comportment," he answered. "You comport yourself like teachers I had in school."

She looked at him with a suspicious gaze, as though perhaps she didn't know what "comportment" meant. Or maybe she had perceived he was not entirely sober. Whichever, Jake saw she did not seem to care for his input, and she looked away from him and back to Jordan as though Jake were yesterday's mackerel. Jordan said:

"How long will you be here?"

"We go home tomorrow. Three months we've been here."

"You must like Mexico."

"We love it here," she said, and both Jordan and Jake looked to the old guy across from her. But he gave no input on that topic either, so they had to assume she spoke for him well and truly, and that he, too, loved being in Mexico.

Jordan ordered another beer. After again watching the way the patrona moved inside her jeans, they heard the lady from Boston saying:

"You haven't touched your food. Look at that. I take you out and you don't eat. How do you expect to get better if you don't eat? And when was the last time you did your exercises? When was the last time I saw you do this?" She raised her hands over her head and lowered them to her lap three times in succession. "Why don't I see you exercising?"

Jordan lisped out past his gold tooth: "She's a Jew, isn't she?"

Jake shrugged. "We know she's a bitch."

"That's a hex around her neck, no?"

Jake now noticed her silver Star of David hanging from a chain necklace. "Is this significant?"

Jordan drank off his beer, keeping his attention focused on the Magen David. "The Mormons believe the Aztecs were the lost tribe of Israel. I'm formulating a new theory of marriage vis-à-vis Jews, Aztecs, and owners of Mexican seafood restaurants."

Jake saw that Jordan was just as not entirely sober as he was.

"Henry, you pay the bill," the old woman said as she pushed up from the card table, and the old man starting leaning to the side as though reaching for his wallet. But he did not reach for it and kept tilting and tilting until the chair slid out from beneath him and he fell to the concrete floor with a plopping sound, like mud.

The owner had run down the block and come back with a young, bearded doctor carrying a black leather bag. The doc seemed a little shaken by the scene, as though unaccustomed to death. He took out his stethoscope, listened for a heartbeat, then turned white-faced to Jordan and Jake.

"Muerto!" he gasped.

"Thus the lack of input," Jordan murmured sotto voce.

Then the young doctor took a small mirror from his bag, held it over the old guy's lips, then studied it. He looked straight at Jake and moved his head slowly from side to side.

"Está muerto."

Finally he took a penknife from his pocket, jabbed the dead man's palm twice, and shrugged. "Muerto," he said falsetto.

The ambulance attendants had shown up by then. They apparently saw no point in dirtying a clean sheet on a corpse and so loaded him on the cart as he was, staring in the same vacant way he had been since he first sat down.

The old lady sat on a folding chair in the corner, staring dumbly with her mouth open, as though mimicking the old man. It seemed she didn't know what to say or, if she did, now had no one to say it to.

The ambulance attendants wheeled the body out with the old lady following as though in a trance. Jordan gazed at the corpse rolling by, staring back at him beseechingly, and suddenly he clapped his hands and yelled:

"Mostaza de los alemanes!"

Jake looked at him as though Jordan were pasado, as though he had finally gone irrevocably beyond sanity.

"Mostaza alemana," Jordan repeated. "German mustard. Horseradish, man." And again he clapped his hands. "Ándale!"

They called the patrona over for another beer, and another, and spent the next hour discussing what made Jordan think of it just then.

Chapter

SIX

It was a Monday morning, and the sun was shining, and Jake felt good until he ran into Jordan in the zócalo. Jordan had just come from the post office and was upset because his monthly government check still hadn't arrived.

"It should have been here last week. I think they're stealing my checks."

"Who?"

"The people in the post office."

"Seems far-fetched, even for Mexico."

"You can't trust anybody," he said, then hit Jake up for twenty pesos. Jake thought it a quaint way to ask for a loan, but Jordan said he needed it to buy some oils, so he gave it to him.

As Jordan folded the money away in his shirt pocket, he said, "By the way, your name's on the lista de correo."

They shook hands, and Jake went to the post office to see

who could be writing him general delivery. The folks in the States whom he wanted to hear from had his address; his acquaintances in Mexico could find him in the zócalo—though that now seemed a mixed blessing. Damn Jordan.

At the post office Jake checked the list taped to the wall and found his name, as Jordan had said. The clerk rifled a stack of letters that he kept under the counter and after a moment handed Jake a picture postcard. Jake recognized the scene as the pyramids of Monte Albán, shot through the branch of a flowering tree that had apparently been held in front of the lens to frame the photo.

He knew Monte Albán, the deserted city—abandoned first by the Zapotecs then by the Mixtecs—that sat in the clouds above the valley of Oaxaca. A magical, holy city, some believed, where gods once lived but now only tourists visited. He carried the card outside before turning it over, trying to figure out who could be writing him from Oaxaca. He had no good guesses and flipped it over.

When he saw the signature and read the brief message penned in a polished hand, a smile came to his face. Jake was surprised to hear from Arthur, surprised that Arthur would write him, of all people. He hadn't been one of his close friends and hadn't thought about him for months, not since Arthur first disappeared. Yet Jake suspected this was the first anyone there had heard from him. For during his last few months in town, Arthur had walked under a cloud. It was, in a way, a cloud of his own making, but he also had a lot of help.

Arthur had been pretty typical of the small group of permanent gringo residents in town: retired, sober, cautious, insular. Perhaps a bit less insular than others. He'd been a teacher and so volunteered at the local secondary school giving English lessons.

Most of these Americans—at least the men, whom Jake knew better than their wives—had lived through the Depression, fought in World War II or Korea, and possessed few of the doubts or neuroses of Jake's generation. You pulled your share and followed the rules; you minded your own business and kept within bounds. Which meant you might have an occasional Mexican friend and you drank with the Mexicans at the American Legion, but mostly you kept to your own kind. That attitude certainly didn't help Arthur's problem, but it would have been a problem anyway. Jake now recalled the first inkling he had of it.

It had been another sunny morning, and he was sitting in the zócalo taking it in when he overheard two gray-haired gringos with tennis racquets talking on the next bench. Jake had no desire to eavesdrop but couldn't help it. That was another thing the older gents had in common: volume.

". . . When I stopped by his place at the usual time, he wasn't ready. Came to the door in his robe, looking like he just got out of bed. Said he'd meet us."

"Think he's okay?"

"I think he's diddling the maid."

"Didn't know you could have a maid in an RV."

"Well, when he opened the door . . . Tell you later. Here he comes now."

Up sauntered Arthur with his tennis racquet, beaming, looking fit, as always. He waved to Jake and stopped in front of the tennis players.

"Let's go. I don't have all day. Get off your asses, and let's play some tennis."

That kind of talk was typical as well. Lots of self-satisfied wisecracking and irony. But the comment about the maid came back to Jake the next week at Jordan's opening.

Jordan had managed to finish enough canvases for a show in Mexico City but needed to finance it. The gallery there wanted some front money for publicity, and there would be frames, transportation, a hotel room, et cetera. So he figured to do a show at the local crafts gallery first and sell a few pictures to the old gringos or Mexican tourists. Jake figured he'd be lucky to sell anything locally, but Jordan didn't ask his opinion.

The cocktail opening turned out to be a typical expatriate community affair: Mexican girls carrying around trays of wine glasses with a short measure of Mexican plonk; a few local dignitaries, that is, Jordan's creditors, seeing if anything sold; and the gringos, tightfisted retirees who would never ever loan an artist a dime but who would come for the free drinks and chit-chat and might just buy something for over the sofa if the wine got to them. Jake was there both as creditor and gringo, trying to drink off the debt, figuring it to be the one and only installment he'd ever see from Jordan.

More people turned out than Jake would have thought, whatever their motives. He and Jordan were leaning on the bar when they saw Arthur come in with her. She was twentyish, not tall, but had a nice face and pleasant smile. Arthur worked toward the bar, grinning and introducing her on the way. When he got there he said in slow, distinct, Voice-of-America English:

"Esperanza, I'd like you to meet the artist, Mr. Jordan Trice Freeman. Jordan, this is my student, Esperanza Arenas Contreras."

"My pleasure, Miss Arenas," Jordan said.

"Pleas-ed to meet you, Mr. Trice."

Jake caught Arthur's eye, and Arthur gave him a shrug: So she needed a little work. Jordan very politely explained to her in English, and again in Spanish so he was sure she understood, about patronymics and matronymics in northern European versus Latin American cultures. When Jordan finished, Arthur introduced Jake.

"I thought this would be a good chance for Esperanza to try out her English in a social situation."

Jake shook her hand and said:

"This is a perfectly social situation—as opposed to a commercial situation. See the pained expressions on the faces of Jordan's creditors? It is entirely too social for their tastes. But the hell with them. Let's be social and have a drink."

They each took a glass of wine. Jordan said:

"How about a painting for your RV, Arthur? Any wall space between the tennis racquets? We've a special tonight on eighteen-by-twenty-fours with frames to match any decor. What do you say?"

Jake saw that Esperanza was looking at Jordan with a fixed smile that said she had no idea what he was talking about. Arthur, too, was smiling. He was always smiling.

"I say you two are pretty damn social. So social that you'd fall over if you didn't have the bar to lean on. I think we'll take a look at the paintings."

He waved to them and led Esperanza away, where she might have a better shot at social conversation. They watched them move off, and Jordan said:

"A pretty girl."

It was then Jake remembered what he'd heard in the zócalo the week before about Arthur being in bed with someone. But Esperanza seemed an unlikely candidate. After all, she was young and beautiful, and he was an old man.

But apparently he had it figured wrong.

A few days later Jake was up early as usual and at the Café Cristóbal Colón, where he drank coffee every morning and scribbled away in his journal. Arthur entered in his tennis whites, racquet in hand and Esperanza in tow. Jake stood and shook hands with them both before they took a table near the door.

They ordered breakfast, and Jake watched them surreptitiously as he wrote. They talked incessantly, and he heard bits of both Spanish and English floating over to him. They also seemed to laugh a lot.

But shortly, Jake got interested in his journal and forgot about them until Arthur stood, gave Esperanza some money for the bill, took up his racquet. It was then that Jake saw her reach up from beneath the table, where she had kept her hands folded in her lap, and squeeze Arthur's free hand. She did it quickly and shyly, and Jake was the only one to see it. A small gesture, but it struck him. And he wondered later if it didn't figure into what he did.

Soon Jake began hearing the talk, or overhearing it, first from Arthur's tennis partners in the zócalo.

". . . You'd never guess who Arthur took to dinner last night at the Stein's."

"Well, they're shacked up, aren't they? He can't leave her alone in the trailer every night."

"You should have seen Ruth Stein's face when they walked through the door. Then I get an earful from my wife when we get home, all about older men lusting after young girls. I couldn't tell if she was disappointed in Arthur or me or men in general."

"She's been disappointed in you for years."

"Esperanza. That's the girl's name: Hope."

"High hope!"

"High hopes for Arthur!"

They laughed about it, but for Arthur it was getting serious. A few days later Jake found him in the cafe with Jordan, and they waved him over. As he sat, Jordan was saying:

"She's going to fleece you, man. How old is she?"

Arthur shrugged. "Twenty-two."

"And how old are you?"

"Sixty-one—no, sixty-two."

"Does her family have any money?"

"Nada. One of ten kids, the father's a pharmacist, and her mother keeps getting pregnant."

"She's a very pretty young woman."

"I think so."

"She could have any guy in town, right? She's after your money."

Arthur pressed his bottom lip between thumb and forefinger and stared through the open door into the street. Although he was among those who wouldn't loan Jordan a cent, he would listen to him. It cost nothing to listen.

"Maybe you're right. Maybe money's important to her. She's never had anything. But still, if she makes me happy . . ."

"You're happy because you think you can trust her. You think she's not going to run around on you. But she's young. She's going to make you miserable, Arthur. And she's going to make you pay through the nose."

Arthur had nothing to say in response to that. Jake didn't say anything either, although he wasn't in total agreement. He also had some thoughts about trust, and about regret. But no one had asked his opinion, so he didn't offer it.

Finally Jordan gave Arthur a slap on the back.

"It'll work out. Just don't let her make a fool of you."

Arthur nodded. "I'll be careful."

And Jake knew he would. He was that kind of guy.

A few weeks passed in which Jake saw very little of Arthur. But that wasn't particularly odd. Although it was a small town, you could mind your own business and almost disappear. He guessed that was what Arthur was doing. And Jake was doing the same.

Jake had found that sometimes you just get too much of people. You don't want anything to do with anybody, and you disappear into Russia with Turgenev or the Far East with Conrad. Or Mexico. You start listening to yourself instead of others. You wait. That's what he was doing. He even drank alone, or at least where he was likely to meet no one he knew.

Jake had found a cantina down by the bus station that was usually near empty—an occasional passenger waiting for a bus, an occasional whore trying to divert that passenger. That night there seemed to be but a lone customer, a stoic hombre with a cowboy hat, standing rigidly at the bar as though quite drunk. Jake moved to the other end of the bar, got a Victoria from the bartender, and then heard the jukebox click on behind him.

It was one of those norteño love songs with the sad accordion. He turned to see who had played it, and there was Arthur, moving away from the machine and settling down behind a beer on a low bench in the shadows along the wall. Jake carried his beer over to him. When Arthur looked up they shook hands, and the older man nodded toward a chair.

Despite his sixty-two years, Arthur struck most people as an attractive, youthful man. A full head of silver hair parted on the side; a deep tan; a lean, angular build. But tonight he looked his age. It was the hangdog expression and the way his shoulders sagged.

"You do not look a happy man, Arturo. You look like a man who has backed the wrong horse."

Arthur shook his head and laughed a hollow laugh. "It's a one-horse race, Jake, and I'm still losing. And for the first time in my life I don't know what to do about it.

"Up to now it hasn't always been easy, but it's always been clear: What a man ought to do and what he shouldn't. Right and wrong. But now . . . I've gotten into it deep this time, waded right out in the middle."

"Esperanza?"

"Esperanza. She wants to get married. I think the priest put a bug in her ear. Under normal circumstances it would be the right thing to do. But, Jesus, I have a granddaughter her age."

Arthur drained off his beer, and Jake waved to the bartender for two more.

"I called my daughter in San Diego. She was lukewarm about my marrying a Mexican even before she found out Esperanza's age. And then, when I told her . . .

"I'd just be making an old fool of myself. Everyone says so—my daughter, Jordan, everyone. Esperanza's got to be after my money, but who can blame her? Why else would she want to marry me?"

Jake could think of other reasons but assumed the question to be rhetorical. The bartender brought the beers over, and Arthur took a long drink before continuing:

"Now my friends have stopped inviting me. I know it's nothing personal against Esperanza. She just doesn't fit in. I knew it couldn't go on like this, even before the marriage business came up. But now . . . I'm afraid she'll leave me if I say no. And if I say yes, I'm afraid she'll break my heart."

It was tough listening to him. Arthur was a decent guy trying to do the decent thing with Esperanza. And being decent about friends who ostracized him and decent to a daughter who told him he was an old fool. He was being decent to everyone except himself and being too damn decent in general, by Jake's standards. But his standards weren't involved. Jake shook his head in sympathy.

"Yep. Looks like a tough spot."

Arthur stared at his beer bottle and began peeling off the yellow label with his thumb. Then he spoke without looking up.

"You've been around some, haven't you, Jake? I mean with women."

"Somewhat."

"I was married to the same woman for nearly forty years and never strayed. Then, when she was gone, I came down here, and there were one or two gals my own age at first. Americans. But it never seemed right. Then Esperanza came, and I felt happy again. Like I said, all I've known is one good woman—and Esperanza." Arthur peeled off more of the label, then looked up. "What do you think I should do, Jake?"

Jake was surprised that Arthur asked his opinion at that stage. He already had so much fine advice to consider. Also, Jake felt odd being asked about such things by a man his father's age. He took a sip of beer.

"Do you love her?"

Arthur nodded without hesitation. "I love her."

"Do you have air in your tires?"

Arthur squinted at Jake as if he were a bit slow, and Jake went on:

"Take her to the priest, Arthur, put a ring on her finger if that's what she wants, and get your RV on the road."

Arthur sat straight up and looked at Jake as though insulted.

Jake could see that this alternative had never occurred to Arthur. It was not decent or honorable to run from difficulty, even to dodge the people who fabricated the difficulty for you as a personal favor. He could see Arthur needed practice being indecent.

"But what if she's just after my money?"

"What if she isn't? What if she reveres you, in whatever way? And even if she was after your money, it might be worth it. How much time do you have left, Arthur? Yeah, she could break your heart and take your money, but she's going to make you happy for a while, and maybe for a long while."

"But . . ."

"I wouldn't tell anyone, Arthur, not even your daughter. Just get on the road tomorrow and don't stop."

Arthur stared at Jake. But he said nothing in reply, and Jake could see he was thinking about it. He saw that Arthur was picturing it in his mind, imagining it. Jake imagined it, too. He knew that if he ever had the chance again, it was exactly what he'd do.

But that was all months ago, the last he'd seen or heard of Arthur until the postcard. And as he carried the brightly colored picture of Monte Albán across the zócalo, Jake saw Arthur's tennis buddies sitting in their white shorts on the metal park benches, overheard them joking and being ironical. Then he read once again Arthur's brief message:

Dear Jake,

From Monte Albán you can see forever, and all the roads you can take.

Chapter

SEVEN

It rained nearly every afternoon in July and August, great thundering downpours that came from the Pacific and lasted a half hour before pushing on across the high plateau. Yet everyone seemed surprised when they came, and almost no one carried an umbrella.

Jake figured that for the men it was the ever-present machismo factor. An umbrella seemed an Anglo thing that bespoke caution and prissiness. Plus, it usually rained only thirty minutes, so why carry an umbrella all day? Besides, if the rain made you halt for a moment and contemplate the power of nature, so much the better.

That was the way people thought there, and Jake saw that he had been in Mexico perhaps too long, for he had begun to think that way, too. When the clouds opened up each day, he would duck into a doorway or rest under the portales or simply get wet. It was out of his hands. He did not control the rain.

That afternoon he had just returned to town from a walk in the campo and was headed home for siesta when the storm blew in. He saw it coming and walked faster, but when he got near the cathedral on the town square he heard thunder and looked up, and the rain began falling in sheets. Jake hunched his shoulders and jogged toward the zócalo to take cover under the manicured elms with white-painted trunks. But as he stood under the trees, hands in pockets, he heard a crack of lightning. It was then he looked around and saw Sid Stein waving to him from the bandstand at the center of the zócalo.

Jake dashed the few yards to the bandstand and moved up the steps to the covered platform. Sid shook his hand and said something, but with the rain beating on the tin roof, Jake had no idea what he said. Sid took the cigar from his mouth.

"Some rain. Not like back home."

Jake nodded agreement. That was the one thing he and Sid had in common: St. Louie. Jake had come from there once, and Sid had been in business there before retiring and moving to Mexico, so that's what they talked about if they happened to meet in the zócalo or at a party. But Jake usually avoided parties where retired gringos like Sid were invited and kept clear of most of the few Americans in town. If he had wanted to be around Americans, he would have stayed home.

"Rains like crazy, and there's never enough water. You'd think they'd build a dam." Sid shook his head and looked at a young Indian woman standing next to him nursing an infant she carried in her rebozo. "They're like children, these people."

"It's refreshing."

Sid looked up at the sky, misconstruing Jake's remark.

"Yes, but every day?"

The noise of the rain made conversation difficult, and Jake was content to wait out the storm in silence. He saw that the woman with the child was no more than fifteen or sixteen. She stared at the downpour without expression. Neither did she control the rain. Sid said:

"Look. There's that crazy colored guy. Not sense enough to come in from the rain."

Jake looked up and saw Jordan moving deliberately through the zócalo, bareheaded, hands in the pockets of a black nylon windbreaker that had been soaked through. Jordan seemed to feel their eyes on him and turned, and when he saw Jake he changed direction and came toward the bandstand.

Jake and Jordan shook hands. Jordan's faded, paint-smeared jeans had been darkened by rain.

"You've got to help me out."

Jake wondered how much Jordan would hit him up for this time.

"My brother died. My younger brother. I've got to get back to New York and straighten things out."

"Sorry. How old was he?"

"Four years younger. That bitch wife of his will sell off all my paintings. I need five hundred bucks."

Sid was staring off in the other direction as if studying the rain, puffing on his cigar, but Jake could tell he was listening.

"Can't you just call someone there to take care of it?"

"I don't need advice, man. I need some fucking money. What do you say?"

"Sorry."

"You got the money, I know it. I need it. I've got to get my stuff. I'll pay you back next month."

That was a lie, and they both knew it. Jake had given him money before, a few pesos here or there to buy paints or food, knowing he'd never see it again, despite Jordan's promises to repay. But Jordan had always been square on why he wanted it.

Now, however, Jake questioned Jordan's reason to leave so abruptly. He had boasted he hadn't been to the States in twenty-five years. Paintings stored with his brother all that time seemed an unlikely lure, if they in fact existed. But ultimately it made no difference what Jordan's motivations were. Jake wasn't about to throw away that much money.

"I can't. You'll have to find it somewhere else."

Jordan moved closer, arms held rigid at his sides. He threw a glance at Sid and sneered at Jake. "You white folks take and take and never give. No generosity, no humanity. You might as well be dead."

Jake had to smile at that after all the breakfasts and beers Jordan had mooched off him.

"I hope you're not threatening me," Jake said, and paused there.

He did not want to fight. The police station was right there on the zócalo, and they'd both spend a night in the bote and have to buy their way out the next morning. Also, an afternoon fistfight in the town square would give the Mexicans a bad impression of Americans, and they had had enough already. Still, he couldn't let it pass.

Jordan seemed to relax and said:

"I just need some fucking money."

"Then do what I did: earn it. Sell some paintings."

Jordan snorted, turned on his heel, and went down the bandstand steps two at a time.

When he had disappeared into the rain, Jake lit up a Faro and looked at Sid. "I apologize for not introducing you."

Sid smiled and shook his head.

"They're animals, I tell you. Animals. They'd come into my store and steal and spit on the floor. Animals."

The two men smoked in silence and watched the rain. After a moment Sid leaned toward Jake and touched his hand.

"I had a friend with a shop on Delmar Boulevard. They came in at closing as he was emptying the register. Came in with guns and tied up both him and his wife. They took his wife and made him watch. Both of them. Then they made her go down on them. He had to watch it all." Sid lifted his hand from Jake's. "Animals, I tell you, animals."

Jake looked up at the sky and waited for the rain to stop.

There was still some light in the sky, and Jake found the address without trouble. He rang the bell, and a young Indian girl opened the door for him. But once inside the outer wall, when he saw the rambling house with the satellite dish on the roof, he wished he had been more assertive when Sid had invited him to dinner. Instead he had readily consented, though his heart wasn't in it.

Jake followed the girl down a walk to the main house and inside to a large sala with a polished stone floor and gaping fireplace. Three other couples were gathered around it, and Jake was glad he wasn't alone with Sid and his wife.

". . . You should have seen it. Fires everywhere, looting, beatings, shooting. And why? What do they gain?" Sid spread his hands. "Someone tell me what they gain. No, they lose. And where are the police? Where are they hiding? . . . Come, come, Jake. Come and meet everyone."

Jake recognized the faces of two of the men, whom he had seen in the zócalo in their tennis shorts. He shook hands all around, and Sid called over a middle-aged maid who had been standing beside the fireplace.

"Whiskey and soda para el señor."

When Sid turned back to him, Jake said:

"Did I miss something?"

"You didn't hear about the riots over the weekend?"

Jake shook his head. It must have been a week since he'd seen a newspaper. Nothing happening anywhere else on earth had much effect on his life in Mexico. Occasionally he bought an *Excelsior* to see what was going on in the world, or the English-language *News* to check the National League standings.

"It was everywhere—L.A., New York, Chicago."

"What was it all about?"

"Who knows?"

Sid's wife, Ruth, said:

"The television would like you to believe it's our fault. That we made them loot and murder and rape. They say it's poverty. Well, my parents were poor; so were Sid's. Did they go riot? No, they went to work."

"Permissiveness," said a bald man on the sofa, one of the tennis players. Tom. "Permissiveness and drugs. No authority, no law. They're all hopped up on drugs and stealing to support their habit."

"They're animals. First the government robs you and then pays people to have babies who grow up to rob you. And the rules and regulations . . ." Sid threw his hands up and lowered them. "It's not worth your time to be in business."

"That's not the U.S.A. I know. It's anarchy," Tom said. "We had burglars three times and said the hell with it. Cops acted like we were making it up. Didn't have time for it. I'll never go back. Never. Used to be a great place. Till they fucked it up. Is this what we fought for?"

"You can't get good people," said Sid, "and a salesclerk wants to be paid like a lawyer. And what you pay for domestics there— ten times what I pay her, and they still can't speak English."

"Enforce the law, that's what I say." This from Tom's wife. "People will do whatever you let them get away with. That's human nature. But we don't enforce the law in the black neighborhoods. No one cares if they kill each other. The police don't care. Can you imagine if there were drugs and gangs in Winnetka? They'd call out the National Guard."

Sid said: "How can you have law with animals? They're not like us, I tell you."

He looked at Jake as though for agreement and support, but Jake said nothing. He figured Sid had been reading too many newspapers, watching too much TV.

Jake didn't run into Sid over the next few weeks and didn't think about the Steins at all. Except for the day that the ambulance came next door.

Jake had just awakened from his siesta and lay on his bed listening to the rain on the roof when he heard a siren growing louder and louder until it seemed as if it were just on the opposite side of the wall. When it stopped, another began in the distance and approached, and Jake got up to see what was going on.

He held his canvas jacket over his head, stepped outside to the terrace, and moved toward the front of the house. When he looked down to the street, Jake saw a police car and an ambulance, both double-parked. The red and blue lights atop the Cruz Roja van were still flashing, and its windshield wipers kept beating back and forth, but he could see there was no one in the front seat.

As he turned and walked back toward his door, a scream cut through the sound of the rain falling to earth. Then again. Jake jogged toward the far end of the terrace and looked down into the patio of the adjoining walled home. There Chief of

Police Muñoz, his beige uniform soaked brown with rain, stood with his hands on the shoulders of a woman wearing a long black braid down her back, as if restraining her. It was she who was screaming.

"Porqué? Porqué? Porqué?"

That was all Jake was able to make out. He saw an open door on one of the makeshift apartments in back, and that seemed to be where the woman was trying to get. A few seconds later two ambulance attendants came out of the open door rolling a cart between them. On it a white sheet covered the form of a body.

When she saw it, the woman broke free from Muñoz, ran to the cart, and pulled back the sheet. Underneath lay a young woman, Jake saw. He looked at her and knew the face, and in a moment remembered the girl who had answered the door at the Steins' and led him down into the sala. Jake reached to hold onto the low wall.

The woman was crying and screaming, "Porqué, Luisa, porqué?" And when Muñoz pulled her from the dead girl and she turned and clung to him, Jake recognized the Indian woman who'd made drinks and served dinner at the Steins'.

His jacket was soaked through. Jake went back inside and sat with the door open, looking at the rain, waiting for it to end so he could go somewhere else.

The rainy season should have stopped at the end of the month. That's what everyone was saying. But it kept on, with violent storms scudding across the mesa each afternoon.

At a table near the door of the Café Cristóbal Colón, Jake ate his comida and watched a great wave of sudden rain beat on the cobbled street. Lightning cracked overhead in the black afternoon sky and rumbled in the distance, and Jake saw people running down the street and squeezing together in doorways for cover. A tall man holding a tennis racquet over his head stepped dripping through the open door of the restaurant, and Jake saw it was Tom in his tennis whites.

He shook water from his arms and lifted his chin at Jake.

"Thought I'd be home by now. Didn't make it."

"Might as well sit and have some coffee. Could be a while."

Tom sat. When the waiter came over he ordered a beer. Jesús brought him a Bohemia and poured Tom a short glass. Tom took a sip and stared at his glass.

"Good beer. They do make good beer here. That's one thing they do better."

"Yes, they do that better."

There was a silence between the two men for a while, then Jake said:

"How's Sid? Haven't seen him in a month."

Tom looked up and licked his lips. After a moment he shook his head slowly and said:

"Gone."

"Dead?"

"No, no. He and Ruth packed up and left. For good. Sold their house and moved to Florida."

A car raced past outside, its tires slapping at the water in the street, and Jake remembered the servant girl—Luisa—being wheeled away in the rain, and he had a sick feeling all over again.

"It was the girl."

Tom nodded. "You heard the whole thing?"

"No. Nothing."

Tom took a long breath and let it out slowly.

"Ruth accused the girl of stealing some jewelry, and the girl hanged herself. Thirteen."

"Good God."

"It was tense up on the hill for a few days. Almost a damn riot over it. The chief of police finally convinced Sid that they would never again be safe here. Damn thing was, it wasn't even her but her girlfriend who took it."

Jake had nothing to say. Tom sipped his beer.

"Tough for Ruth. And Sid. And after everything else they've been through."

Jake knew he wouldn't enjoy hearing it, but he asked anyway. "I guess I don't know what they've been through."

Tom leaned closer. "Sid talks about it sometimes like it was nothing. But you can tell they're not very balanced about it. . . . At their store in St. Louis, a couple black guys came in and robbed them after hours. Raped Ruth and made Sid watch and God knows what else. That's when they packed it in and came down here. No, I don't think they're very balanced."

"No, I see that now. No balance."

The rain stopped as quickly as it had begun, and the sudden quiet made both men look outside through the doorway.

The water running six inches deep in the gutters sounded good to Jake. The rain cleansed the streets and made the air smell fresh. It was all clean and open and quiet to Jake, and it reminded him of a place in the past, a place he now sought to recall but could not grasp.

Chapter

EIGHT

Jake held his hand tight against his side as he moved down the street past the market, ducking under the canvases strung over the stalls of fruits and vegetables to guard them from the morning sun. The hand hurt like hell when he touched it against anything at all, so he held it to his abdomen for protection. But the jolts from walking over the cobblestone street were sufficient to remind him of what he had done to himself—and his motivations, which were none too flattering.

However, he understood that at times like those he was not himself, though he wasn't sure why. But he did suspect that what seemed like reasons for his state of mind were not causes at all, but effects. He figured that when the mood was coming on and before he consciously realized it, his subconscious thoughts started moving toward the blackness, like errant birds that sense a coming earthquake.

Jake had learned that you can live successfully for a time with fixed ideas about yourself and the world, beliefs that grow so familiar and comforting they become like an old friend or a trusted lover—who then betrays you. Except, Jake saw, it's all your own doing, and you do it exceptionally well. You set yourself up and kid yourself and then betray yourself better than anyone else could do it for you.

For example, on day one a man can believe himself enriched and buoyed by an exotic expatriate existence, a life of valuable new perspectives and experience. And on day two—without the facts of this existence altering in any way whatsoever—see himself as a feckless and cowardly fool frittering away his best years in a dead-end detour from his life. Same man, same life; two different days, two different worlds. And that second world replete with self-pity. Let us not forget the self-pity, Jake reminded himself.

It was that sort of sudden clarity the previous night—and a few drinks—that made him take a poke at a scorpion on the brick wall of his room and crack up his hand.

The drinks helped him sleep that night, but the next morning his left hand was swollen and throbbing, and he could not move the last two fingers. The only real doctor he knew in town—and he'd met him but once under hardly social circumstances—had a clinic over by the mercado, down the street from the seafood restaurant where the old gringo dropped dead while Jake was having a beer. The restaurant owner had run down the street and come back with a bearded médico who seemed a little put out about having to minister to a corpse right after dinner. But that recommended him to Jake: a doctor unaccustomed to and offended by death.

Jake found his clinic in the next block down from the sea-food joint. A sign hung over the sidewalk:

DR. JULIO LOURDES, PLASTIC SURGEON

In English yet.

He stepped inside under the sign and found it was a slow morning at the clinic. The nurse—she wore a white dress, at least—immediately showed him into an examination room where Doctor Lourdes sat with his feet up on a desk, drinking coffee and reading a Mexico City newspaper. He glanced over the top of the paper at Jake, who held up the swollen hand. Lourdes shifted his eyes back to the newspaper.

"And what have we been doing?"

"We have been punching out scorpions."

Lourdes dropped the newspaper and nodded toward a chair by the desk. Jake sat, and the doctor stood over him, manipulat-ing his fingers and pressing the back of his hand. When Jake winced, Lourdes smiled.

"Boxer's break."

"You should see the scorpion."

Lourdes looked down at his patient, shook his head, and tapped a cigarette pack in Jake's shirt pocket with the backs of his fingers.

"Bad for the complexion. Give me your smokes, gringo."

Jake handed them to him, and Lourdes lit one up and took a sip of coffee.

"You'll need a half cast."

"You sure it's broken?"

Lourdes brought out a stethoscope from the pocket of his white lab coat and began thumping Jake's chest and listening.

"Being a country doctor is more art than science. You tap, you listen. You touch, you divine."

On the wall behind the desk Jake noticed a framed parchment, an M.D. from Stanford, and his English was good.

"So there is no X-ray machine."

"In Santa Ana. Fifty kilometers. But it's not necessary." The cigarette in the corner of his mouth moved up and down as he spoke, dusting his white lab coat with gray ashes. "A little local anesthetic and a little luck and you'll be like new. Or close."

Lourdes began filling a syringe from a vial on a table by the sink.

"How long for the cast?"

"Four weeks. Six weeks. Who knows?"

Jake was shaking his head as the doctor turned around. "A stupid thing to do. Damn stupid and pointless."

Lourdes stuck the needle into the thick part of the hand. "Perhaps it will be a blessing."

"It will have to improve."

"The turning point in my life was a broken leg. I had thought I would pitch for the Giants until I snapped my left fibula." He made a pitching motion. Lourdes was a southpaw. "It forced me to use my brain instead of my arm, which I now see was but a minor-league arm."

Jake could no longer feel the needle going in, and he glanced about the office as the doctor continued talking and jabbing him with the syringe. The walls needed paint, and the few pieces of furniture seemed worn. Other than the Stanford diploma, there was nothing that said Lourdes was doing any better than a minor-league pitcher.

"Hold it like this, hombre."

Jake put his elbow on the desk and held his hand vertical. Lourdes began pressing to line up the pieces of bone. The doctor grimaced, and Jake heard grinding noises coming from his hand that made him glad for the anesthetic. After a few minutes Lourdes was satisfied.

"Good enough."

The nurse came in to help with the cast. When they were finished, Jake stood and flexed his elbow a few times.

"Feels pretty good."

"Wait till tonight."

"How much do I owe you?"

Lourdes shook his head and waved away the question. "Bring me a bottle of Cognac sometime."

He gave Jake the address where he lived.

Jake was about to walk out when he recalled. He turned and asked:

"Doc, remember that old gringo who died in the mariscos place last month?"

Lourdes nodded and gave a little shudder.

"What was it? What'd he die of?"

Lourdes shrugged as he lit another Faro from the confiscated pack and made a flicking motion with his hand.

"Se fue."

It took itself away, Jake translated. Jake wasn't sure if it was what the doctor intended, but Lourdes seemed to suggest that living, not death, was some sort of aberration.

One evening the next week Jake carried a bottle of Cognac to the address Lourdes had given him. He set the bottle on the stone sidewalk and knocked with his good hand.

It had taken him a couple days to find a bottle of real French Cognac in town. Jake figured Mexican Cognac was not the same thing. He knocked again, and when the door finally opened Lourdes stood there with a blank look on his face. Then he remembered.

"Ah, the scorpion boxer. Pásale."

Above the black beard his face was flushed and his eyes shining. Half his shirttail was out, and Jake saw he did not truly need the Cognac that night.

They stepped into a large, high-ceilinged chamber with old wooden ceiling beams. Lourdes's home was one long room that contained a sala with fireplace, a dining area, and on the other side of the bar, a kitchen. A flight of exposed stairs led to a loft, and a noise there made Jake look up. In the shadows he saw a woman with short blonde hair come out of the bath putting herself together. Off the bedroom there looked to be a rooftop terrace.

Jake paused by the door and said, "If it's not convenient now . . ."

Lourdes put his arm around Jake's shoulder and led him to the bar.

"No, no. Your timing is perfect. Let's have a drink."

He took the Cognac, cut the seal, and poured three small snifters as the blonde came down the stairs. She was something to look at, and Jake did. Everything was just right. She came over and pulled up a barstool, and they shook hands. Lourdes said:

"Elizabeth represents one of my greatest achievements as a plastic surgeon. I may very well make her my poster child."

Jake looked at Elizabeth. Whatever Lourdes had done to her, he had done it well. Her face was smooth and natural, hardly a line in it.

They drank down the Cognac, and Lourdes poured three more. As they again raised their glasses and said, "Salud!" Jake laid his broken hand on the bar. Elizabeth nodded toward the cast.

"What'd you do to it?"

Jake threw a quick combination. "Broke it scorpion-boxing."

"Never heard of that."

She said it with a doubting whine in her voice, and suddenly she didn't look so good.

"It's an up-and-coming sport," Jake said. "A diversion with fast-growing Mexican popularity."

"I went to the cockfights once."

"This is more like bullfighting. Man against nature."

She turned to Lourdes. "Is he for real?"

Lourdes poured down his Cognac. "As physician of record, I can certify that the injury corresponds to one incurred scorpion-boxing."

Jake added: "It's quite a spectacle. You should come see it sometime. You really should."

"I'll make a note."

As the doctor poured more Cognac, Elizabeth realized she'd left her purse upstairs. While she fetched it, Jake said to Lourdes in Spanish:

"You do good work as a plastic surgeon. She looks very beautiful and natural."

Lourdes took the cigarette pack from Jake's shirt pocket and lit up.

"At one time I was considered the best in California. No, in the whole United States of America. 'Surgeon to the Stars.' Sí, Jaque, I do good work."

Elizabeth came back downstairs, and as she again approached the bar, Lourdes stopped her with a gesture before she could sit.

"Elizabeth, show my friend your teats."

Elizabeth yanked up the white ribbed tank top she wore. From five feet Jake could see a faint network of red scar tissue on her otherwise perfect breasts. She moved her shoulders just slightly. She was definitely proud of them.

"Are you a doctor, too?" she asked.

"No, but I'm damn interested."

Lourdes interjected: "You should have seen her, Jake. Lucky to stand up. Tremendous teats. Two, three times this size."

"They look just right. Perfect."

"Oh, thank you," she said, blushing at the compliment and pulling down her top. Jake felt she was warming to him.

Lourdes poured more Cognac, and Elizabeth proposed a toast:

"Here's to perfect tits!"

Lourdes and Jake stood, and the three of them clinked glasses. It was all very festive and ceremonial, and they finished off the bottle of Cognac. But the next day Jake's blackness returned, and he began wondering again what the hell he was doing there. He wondered, too, what Lourdes was doing there. His life seemed no better than Jake's.

After a month the hand no longer hurt when he happened to hit it against something, so he went to see Lourdes at his clinic. Jake hadn't run into him since the night they drank the Cognac. It was a small town, but at times paths did not cross as one thought they should.

Lourdes's nurse asked him to sit and wait. After fifteen minutes, a middle-aged Anglo woman came out of the examination room, and Jake was shown in.

Lourdes looked at the hand, asked if it hurt when he pressed on it, and threw the half cast into the wastebasket.

"Lay off the boxeo for a while, and you'll be fine until arthritis sets in."

"I've retired from the ring."

They smoked a cigarette and talked about the National League. They agreed it wasn't what it used to be.

"There is no pitching today," Lourdes said. "If I were twenty years younger, I could start for the Dodgers. If I had a knuckleball, I could pitch even now. Age is relative, no?"

"You should add that to your sign."

It was then that the nurse came in and begged permission to speak. A man had come to see the doctor. Lourdes told Jake to relax and went out to the waiting room.

Through the open door Jake saw an old campesino holding a straw sombrero in his hands. He couldn't hear what the old man was saying, but after a minute the doctor patted him on the shoulder and sent him away. Then Lourdes came back in and grabbed his valise.

"You have time for a trip to the campo?"

"My calendar is clear."

As they stepped from the clinic into the bright morning sun, Jake realized how true it was. There was nothing on his calendar. He had nothing pressing to do as far into the future as he cared to see.

It was a nice day for a ride: clear skies and crisp mountain air. The highway was smooth. Lourdes drove a battered, topless jeep that had pasted to its windshield a five-year-old parking permit from a San Francisco hospital. Jake lifted his chin toward the permit.

"Is that when you left?"

Lourdes glanced over and nodded. There was no change in his expression, but Jake saw something in his eyes turn inward. Jake was curious but didn't want to ask why he gave it up. Apparently it was something he didn't want to talk about: malpractice, trouble with the law, nervous breakdown. When you asked questions, you never knew whether the answer was going to be something you wanted to hear.

About five miles out of town, Lourdes turned his jeep onto an old cobblestone road that headed off toward pine-covered mountains in the distance and shook the jeep violently. It rattled and vibrated, and the resulting din made conversation impossible. After another mile he turned down a dirt and rock side road.

The road wound by an occasional farmhouse built of irregular stones and through meandering fields of corn. It dipped into dry creek beds and cut between tall palms. They passed two men driving a string of burros and a young girl carrying two black iguanas squirming at either end of a rope.

Shortly the road gave out in a small village where a white stucco church and a score of one-story homes marked the dusty main street. Lourdes moved the jeep down a rutted side street and soon stopped it beside a crude stone home whose doorway was covered by a blue-striped cloth. As they got out, a young woman appeared, lifting the cloth aside.

"Buenos dias, Don Julio. Many thanks for coming. I am very worried about Tomasito."

Lourdes patted her hand. "Tranquila, MariaFelicia. It's okay."

She nodded to Lourdes, then turned to Jake and bowed from the waist. MariaFelicia was dark and Indian with a smooth, handsome face, green eyes, and shining black hair fixed in a single braid that hung to her waist. She had the same spare movements of the campesinas he'd seen at the market, movements that lent her a dignified air.

They followed her inside, where the only light came from an open doorway leading to a garden in back. Lourdes asked MariaFelicia for a lamp, and she brought him a kerosene lantern and matches. As Jake's eyes adjusted from the bright sunshine, he saw that her home was one neat room with a stone floor, a bed in the corner, and a rustic table with two chairs. She carried one of the chairs to Lourdes, who crouched by a wooden cradle near a cold fireplace. The other chair she pulled from the table and offered to Jake, but he shook his head and leaned against the wall.

The child lay silent and motionless in the cradle. Lourdes felt his forehead and lifted him in his arms. "Como estás, Tomasito? Don't you feel well today?"

The mother said: "No llora, no come nada. He does not cry, does not take milk, nothing. There is fever, and he sleeps day and night. I would have waited till Saturday, when you usually come to town, but I was afraid for him. I am sorry to bother you, Don Julio, but I did not want him to become like me."

Lourdes placed Tomasito in the cradle.

"Don't worry, MariaFelicia. These illnesses are normal for a child. But we need to lower the fever."

Lourdes sent her outside for cold water in which to bathe the infant. Jake asked him in English:

"Is he really okay?"

Lourdes came over, clapped him on the back, and took the chair MariaFelicia had offered Jake.

"You don't know about children, do you? Neither does MariaFelicia. This is her first—which I delivered—so she worries. Particularly after what happened to her."

She appeared in the doorway with Tomasito's bath.

"Would the gentlemen like some coffee? Excuse me for not offering before."

They said they would, and she set down the tin basin and went back outside to put on some water. Lourdes shook his head and continued:

"You see unimaginable things in the campo. Things born of superstition and ignorance. People who can't afford medicine but will pay a curandera to cast a spell. Home remedies that do more harm than the injury. And unshakable belief in the efficacy of prayer despite much evidence to the contrary. But MariaFelicia is smart. She has put her faith in Julio Lourdes.

"Her parents, however, were not so wise. When she cried at night as an infant, they used pulque to quiet her. Which it did. But the alcohol also dehydrated her, so that her retinas deteriorated. Thus her blindness. Thus her concern for Tomasito."

"I didn't notice."

"She hides it well."

"She's alone?"

"The husband, Tomás, went to the States to pick apples. He sends money. When they have enough, they'll buy an old pickup and some animals and probably do all right."

MariaFelicia came back in carrying two cups. She set one in front of Lourdes and the other at the end of the table closest to Jake. Then she went to fetch the other chair from beside the cradle, set it before the second cup, and looked up with a smile to where Jake leaned silently against the wall.

Although it wasn't his normal day for that area, Lourdes stopped in to look at other patients on their way back: first an old man who had suffered a compound fracture falling from his burro; then a woman with an infected leg—her dog had knocked over an iron and burned her. The woman with the bad leg sent her son outside to kill a chicken, then fixed dinner for Lourdes and Jake.

The sun was dropping low in the sky when they reached town, and Jake invited Lourdes up for a drink.

They sat in sling chairs on the upstairs terrace outside Jake's room, sipping at a bottle of tequila. But the strong liquor didn't seem right after all the sun and dust. Then Jake saw the maid in the patio below and gave her a tip to go to the tienda down the block for beer.

The sun reached the tops of the black mountains in the distance as they finished a second beer, and Jake handed Lourdes a third. Black grackles streamed overhead toward the zócalo, where they would roost for the night, while great white egrets floated down to tall firs at the bottom of the hill as the sky began turning from royal blue to indigo. A pair of Inca doves fluttered in the avocado tree growing from the patio below.

"You just gave it up, didn't you?"

Lourdes took the beer from Jake and raised it—"Salud!"— then settled back in his chair to watch the sunset. After a moment he said:

"I came home."

He gestured with his beer bottle toward the mountains and the setting sun, now red-orange. The firs below were dark green, the bougainvillea deep magenta; all around them were flowering plants and verdant trees. "It is something, eh, Jaque?"

"It is something indeed," Jake said, and in his mind he saw MariaFelicia holding Tomasito in her eternal night.

Lourdes went on:

"In the States there were occasions—more frequent near the end—when I would stop what I was doing, even in the operating room, and I could hear my father's voice calling from the grave: 'Julio, Julio, tu esqueleto está vivo. Julio Lourdes, your skeleton is alive.'

"But I would have no answer for him. No way to justify how I made use of my little time."

Lourdes took a drink from his beer bottle and held out his empty tequila glass toward Jake.

"But now, Jake, I have an answer for him, and the old bastard leaves me alone."

Jake sat outside long after the sun had set, long after they had finished off the beer and the tequila and Lourdes had gone home to sleep. The Inca doves had gone to sleep, too, and there was no wind.

Jake sat on the terrace and felt the night surround him like a cool, black cloud. The stars, which had begun appearing while the horizon was still red, filled the night. A shooting star cut an arc over the distant black mountains, and Jake wondered whether the meteor had been traveling through space since the beginning of time, now to expire in a brief few seconds of heat and light. It was then that he got up and went inside.

But there, when he reached down and lit the lamp on the nightstand, he started and stepped back.

A scorpion clung to the wall just above his bed. Not the brown kind but a small, white one—the bad kind. He stood there and stared at it, but a few feet away.

Jake could easily have reached out with the book lying on the nightstand and taken care of it. But instead, he pulled the bed out from the wall, checked under the covers before climbing in, and turned off the light.

Chapter
NINE

Jake had already heard about the guy they found in the bathtub with his skull crushed in. Jesús, the waiter at the Café Cristóbal Colón, had mentioned it. Not many details, just that the head had been caved in with a heavy object and the body badly decomposed, since whoever did it had dumped plaster into the dead man's bathwater. The victim had been a sculptor and kept the plaster around for his work; the lime in the plaster had already started working on him by the time his body was discovered.

The description was detailed enough for Jake, given what he himself had already surmised about the murder, and he didn't care to find out any more. But now it looked like he would.

He lit her cigarette and motioned to the bartender for two more beers. She brushed back her brown-black hair with her free hand and went on:

"Yo estaba muy preocupada—I was very worried. No one had seen Pancho for three or four days, and I got no answer when I knocked at his door. So I telephoned his father in Salamanca. But his father told me, 'Don't worry, Marta. This has happened before. You know Pancho with his tequila and his marijuana. He'll show up.'

"But he didn't. When another three days passed, I telephoned again and persuaded his father to come here."

She stopped talking as the bartender approached, set beer bottles in front of them, and took away the empties. He was a good bartender, quietly efficient. Though they were the only customers in the cantina that night, he seemed always to be looking at someone else but noticed immediately whenever Jake motioned for another round.

The cantina itself was less impressive: gritty, unswept floors; water-stained walls; worn wooden chairs whose leather seats had cracked with age. Only the jukebox placed them accurately in time: a shiny, computerized model that took only new pesos, looked like a space capsule, and kept playing compact discs of Mexican torch songs, typical ranchero tunes about unrequited love, death during childbirth, and cruel vendettas. However, Jake saw that the bartender had figured out how to bypass the computer. Whenever the music stopped, he went to the juke, opened the front with a butter knife, and jiggled its inner works. When the music resumed, he would go back behind the bar and continue pretending not to look at his only two customers.

Marta went on:

"When his father arrived in town, we got a key to Pancho's casita from the landlord and went there together. When we opened the door, we knew there had been trouble . . ."

She took a sip of beer and again brushed back her hair, and Jake had the sudden realization that she was preening, that her habit was a self-stroking designed to draw attention to her beauty. And she was a good-looking woman. Jake had seen her around town, usually with a young, bearded Mexican—her fiancé, the dead sculptor Pancho, he now presumed. Jake may even have spoken to her once or twice. But they never got together. Not until now, and this was a seeming fluke.

He had been sitting in the zócalo watching the sunset, and when he looked around she was sitting at the other end of the metal bench. They chatted, and Jake invited her for a drink. But it wasn't until they got to the cantina and had a couple beers that Jake realized she was the woman of the dead man whom Jesús had mentioned and whom Guillermo had apparently killed.

". . . All his work, his sculptures, had been destroyed. They were in pieces, lying in a heap on his bed, and his clothes had been tossed on the floor.

"It was the same in the kitchen. All the dishes had been thrown to the floor, all the cups and glasses, too. Then we went into the bath . . ."

Jake tried to look nonchalant, as though he had heard nothing previously about the incident—just as he had done when Jesús was telling him about it, when he tried to appear calm even when imagining his friend, the dead taxista Guillermo, bludgeoning the sculptor to death. Jake sipped at his beer and nodded. She continued:

"There, too, his things were on the floor. The towels had been thrown into the bathtub, which was filled with soapy water. At least that was how it looked.

"His father shook his head and said: 'Pancho must have done this himself. He must have felt a failure and so destroyed all that he created. Now he is off on a borrachera and will return when he sobers up.'

"We agreed that must have been what happened and decided to put his casita in order for his return.

"I began in the bath, and went to remove the towels from the tub. But as I did, there was something else with them. Piel. Skin. White leather. I began pulling the towels from the water and with them came skin, skin, more skin . . ."

Marta was making grasping motions with her hands and pulling motions with her arms, and Jake saw she no longer looked at him but that her eyes had glassed over and stared at the memory of the thing. Despite not really wanting to hear more, he listened now with great concentration, trying to keep up with her Spanish as it quickened, and he was getting most of it, plenty of it.

". . . Piel, piel, más piel. I kept pulling skin from the white water, and it was on my hands and on my arms and on the floor, and Pancho's father grabbed me to stop me.

"Then he reached carefully into the water, running his hand down the side of the bath to find the plug, and pulled it, and the water began to lower. The water went down inch by inch, and we saw the shape of his body rise through the white water. It was like the sheet you lay over a sleeping child, which floats down flat and smooth, then takes the shape of the child."

Marta paused, lit another cigarette, and poured out the last of her beer. Jake bought her another, then she told him what the body looked like.

Jake woke in the middle of the night and wondered for a moment where he was. Then he remembered.

He sensed the slightest stirring beside him, turned slowly, and saw her, naked and white in a beam of near-full moon that fell through the open window onto the straw mat where they lay. He saw her arms outstretched above her, reaching toward the night sky as she slept, fingers moving serpentlike around one another, as though she were washing her hands in moonlight, again and again, and he saw on her face there sat a soft smile.

Next morning at the Café Cristóbal Colón Jesús brought Jake his coffee and said:

"You seem tired, amigo."

"I did not sleep well," Jake said, and left it at that. He had a headache and did not feel sociable. Certainly he did not feel like talking about the previous night, so he stirred his coffee.

But Jesús did not go away. He stood over him, stood quite still, and when Jake finally looked up, Jesús said:

"Tenga cuidado. Take care, amigo."

"What do you mean?"

"I mean nothing."

"You must mean something."

And the waiter turned and walked away.

Chapter
TEN

Jake ran into Marta as she was coming out of the Farmacia Así Es La Vida studying a packet of birth control pills she had just bought. She slipped the pills into her purse, bit her lip, and told him:

"No tienes obligación."

She said it and smiled—and she had a lovely smile. But he still felt obligated, no matter what disclaimers she made and no matter that he had been to bed with her but once, the previous week. For some said that her fiancé, Pancho, had ended up dead for scorning her.

Nonetheless, despite the rumors about her trepanning Pancho in jealousy, she seemed well-mannered and pacific, with that certain mix of Spaniard and Moor and Aztec that made her dark and compelling in a way no fair woman could ever be. Thus Jake—now discounting her murderous Spanish, Moorish, and Aztec blood—found it hard to believe she had done it. But then he had yet to scorn her or see her angry, and also knew that most people were capable of more than we gave them credit for. Still, he did not think it was she who had done in Pancho. Not really.

She laid her hand on Jake's arm just below the elbow, and he felt a tingle in his stomach. She was quite something to see, yet he could but vaguely recall what she looked like undressed.

"Estás ocupado?"

He shook his head. "No, not right now." It was a town of a certain size and lethargy where no one was ever too busy to accept an invitation, and everyone knew it.

"Then please come with me for coffee."

She took his arm, and they made their way down the block toward the Café Cristóbal Colón, Jake feeling as though he were in protective custody, under arrest, obligated.

When they walked through the open doors of the cafe and saw her uncle Don Pablo Martínez sitting at the corner table from which he ran things in the pueblito, Marta called out, "Tio!" as though surprised to see him sitting where he sat every morning and afternoon, except Sundays.

Don Pablo looked up with a smile but then gave a start when he saw Jake with his niece. It wasn't anything very noticeable, just a slight tightening of the eyes, but Jake noticed it. He guessed that Don Pablo, like most townsfolk there, believed it inappropriate for Mexican maidens to consort with gringos, who were all thought to be on permanent shore leave, more or less. But Don Pablo stood and, after kissing his niece on either cheek, shook Jake's hand and smiled.

"Of course I know your face. I see you at breakfast each morning but have not felt the right to interfere with your work. Please sit, both of you, and join me."

"Gracias, Tio," said Marta.

"Gracias. Very kind," said Jake, and he held Marta's chair for her, then sat across from Don Pablo, who was being awfully nice.

Don Pablo signaled for the waiter, Jesús, and they all ordered coffee. But Jesús, who served Jake breakfast every day and who drank a beer with Jake on occasion, would not look directly at Jake. Everything had now changed. Now that Jake was socializing with Don Pablo, he was no longer just a pinche gringo, that is, a person of no account, but had moved right to the top of the pueblito's social hierarchy. Thus he was someone to whom Jesús had to show deference.

"I have noticed you working, writing in your notebook each morning," said Don Pablo to Jake. "You are writing a book?"

"No. Solamente mi diario, my daily impressions of life in Mexico."

"But certainly the life of our town is very boring compared to life in the United States. Ours is an insignificant pueblito where nothing interesting ever happens."

That Pancho got his skull crushed in and the police shrugged their shoulders when the niece of the most powerful man in town was a logical suspect seemed rather interesting to Jake. But he assumed Don Pablo was referring only to cultural events.

"Yet to someone like myself accustomed to big cities, the life of your pueblito is refreshing. Here everyone knows his neighbor, and friendships are more easily formed." Jake tried not to look at Marta when he said it, but Don Pablo gave her a glance.

"Truly. Here we value friendship highly. I have seen you with the Negro artist, Señor Freeman, a tenant of mine. It is good to have the friendship of countrymen when in a foreign land."

Jake now had the feeling that Don Pablo was speaking in code, that the sudden reference to Jordan had some deeper meaning. But as to what that meaning was, he had no guesses.

"Yes. At times I long for English conversation. For me, Spanish is not easy."

"But your Spanish is quite good. You speak very clearly and without accent."

Jake thanked Don Pablo, who was being too damn nice.

Jesús came with the coffee and still did not look at Jake. Marta talked with her uncle about maiden aunts and far-flung cousins while Jake sipped his coffee.

Jake knew from Jesús that Don Pablo had his finger in most things in town. He knew from Jordan something of Don Pablo's real estate holdings. Don Pablo was a powerful man who needed nothing from Jake, a no-count outsider, yet seemed for some reason to curry his favor. Jake figured it had to be because of Marta.

Marta rose and kissed her uncle's cheek. Jake got up, and Don Pablo got up with him to shake his hand again.

"Much pleasure to know you."

"The pleasure is mine."

"Some morning when you have time, I would like to hear what you have to say about our town in your journal."

Jake doubted very much that Don Pablo would like some of his observations. He said:

"It is a beautiful town, a magical place."

"How true," said Don Pablo, and as he laid his hand on Jake's shoulder, Jake realized that whatever anonymity he thought he possessed in the backwater pueblito no longer existed, if it ever had. Don Pablo had many eyes, eyes everywhere in town. And now, perhaps at Marta's urging, Don Pablo had taken an interest in Jake. But it was not attention he wanted or deserved.

He'd slept with her only once. And he had no plans to do it again and get more deeply involved.

Once outside the cafe, when they had moved down the block out of her uncle's view, Marta stood on tiptoes, kissed Jake's chin, and whispered in his ear:

"Me encantas. Me cambias.—You enchant me. You change me."

And as he smelled her scent, felt her warm breath in his ear, and saw a look of solicitation in her eyes, his independent intentions were spirited away like dust blown across the high mesa.

They crossed the patio of the house where Jake rented a room on the roof and passed the middle-aged gringa who had taken a room downstairs. She sat in a sling chair in the garden, wearing a broad-brimmed straw hat to protect her pale skin and a flowered skirt. She looked up and tried to smile as they passed, but it was not a good effort.

In his room he poured two shots of tequila from a bottle he kept on the mantel over the fireplace. Marta leaned toward him, and they kissed and drank down the tequila. Jake sat on the bed. She stood at the end of it and slid her white jeans down over her hips, and he focused on her long, brown legs. She stood there—silver earrings peeking through long, near-black hair— in a silk turquoise blouse and a black bikini. She unbuttoned the blouse, and he saw a silver necklace on her brown chest and dark brown aureoles on her breasts. Jake lay back on the bed and watched.

It was all new to him. The first time had been at night, in moonlight, and they had drunk some. The lovemaking was unsubtle, and it might have been anyone. Now, as he looked at her dark eyes and straight black-brown hair and the way she moved, he suddenly saw another woman. It was not someone he wanted to see, but there she was, and as Marta came to him, along with her came all the old feelings for the other woman. The feeling of being young and foolish, of being entranced and star-crossed. It was she, reincarnate, and Jake felt as though the gods were giving him a second chance—or mocking him.

She came to him, and he felt her flesh in his hands, tasted her skin, and felt her body against his. Flesh against flesh, and none of the rest seemed to matter. Not the striving or the regrets or the dumb mistakes, nothing. This moved him beyond all that, beyond himself, and he saw all the wasted nights alone. She moved against him with her smooth brown legs and pressed her mouth to his, and for a moment he didn't give a damn about the past. Of course he would again, as soon as it was over, but he didn't think about that now. He moved on top of her, and the silver necklace lay across her throat, and he saw it pulse, and she said:

"Así, así! Thus, thus!"

A ray of afternoon light came through a slit in the homemade curtains and fell dust-flecked across the bed. He drew his fingers up the back of her leg as she lay next to him, up the back of her thigh and buttock, up her spine to her ear, and with her head on the white pillow she smiled at him.

"No lo hago con todo el mundo," she said. "I do not do this with everyone, and never like this, in daylight, without shame. Before, there was but one . . ."

"Pancho."

She shook her head. "No. Never with Pancho. But with the boy I loved when I was still a girl. My family suspected us and sent me away, to study art in Guadalajara and live with my cousins. Likewise the engagement with Pancho. It was an affiancing of families, not lovers."

"Then why me? You did not know me when we first made love."

Jake saw her color. This was not the same woman from the first night. She was more like the ghost woman from his past.

"One cannot explain such things. I had seen you about the pueblito, always alone. And even when I was engaged to Pancho, I would think of you instead of him. Perhaps we were lovers in another life."

Perhaps so, thought Jake. It had seemed that way to him, too, but in a different sense. She saw him thinking about it and asked:

"What are you thinking?"

He did not want to talk about past mistakes, so he moved his thoughts elsewhere. "I have a question."

"Please ask. I wish to hide nothing from you, Jaque. Since now we are lovers, we must have no secrets."

"Tell me then, Marta, why your uncle, Don Pablo, now shows such kindness toward me when for months he did not so much as look in my direction."

Jake saw that his instinct for finding exposed nerves in a woman and saying the exact wrong thing at the right moment was still intact, for Marta suddenly looked away and folded her hands, showing that this was one secret she took no joy in sharing with her lover. Jake waited silently for the experience of sharing. Finally she said:

"He respects you."

Jake shrugged. "He does not know me or anything about me. Why should he have respect for me?"

She turned her back to him, lying on her side, and after a long moment said to the wall:

"Because of what one believes one has done."

She turned back and went on:

"Maybe it is not true. One only believes it is thus. And now that you and I are together, it only makes one have more suspicions. Yet it is not important whether one believes it true or not or what one has done, but only that we are together."

When she had finished and lowered her eyes, Jake looked at her, trying to see what the hell she was talking about. Spanish was a language where no one had to take responsibility for anything. If you wanted, you could attribute all the evil in the world to indefinite pronouns.

"Por favor, Marta, tell me straight what you mean. Why does Don Pablo respect me?"

"He only believes it is thus, and . . ."

"Tell me why."

Finally she looked up. "For assassinating my fiancé."

Jake laughed, even though he did not find it funny.

"En serio? Your uncle truly believes this?"

"Seriously."

"Why would he believe that? For what reasons?"

She shook her head as if she didn't know or as if she didn't want to talk about it, and asked:

"Tienes cigarros?"

Jake fetched a pack of Faros from the pocket of his shirt, which lay on the chair next to the bed, and offered her one. He took one himself, and they lit up.

She sat on the bed, legs crossed, the white sheet drawn across her lap but otherwise naked. Her coffee-colored hair hung straight to her shoulders, the silver earrings showing through it.

Jake saw that she was not going to answer. But he was figuring it out for himself. She already had it all figured out.

"Lo crees, Marta?"

When she did not move, he repeated: "Do you believe it, Marta? Do you believe I killed your fiancé?"

"No importa."

"Yes, it is important," Jake said, and he saw just the faintest sign of pleasure on her lips, as though she was restraining a smile, and he realized what a romantic notion it must be for her.

"No importa," she repeated, and kissed him, pressing her body against his, and he stopped talking.

He heard Taide, the maid, in the patio below with her broom, sweeping, sweeping, and he thought of Pancho lying dead in his bath, his bleached skin separating from his decomposing flesh. But soon the image of the dead fiancé and the sound of the broom slipped from Jake's conscious thoughts, and all that was left was the two of them in bed.

Chapter

ELEVEN

Sharon Olmstead woke early, as usual, and lay in bed staring at the ceiling until the sun was up and shining. Then she rose and opened the shutters of the sole window in her room to a blue sky, red geraniums in the window box, and the pale purple flowers of the jacaranda tree growing outside her door. What she would have given back then, in those years of long, gray, Wisconsin winters, for such color, or even to see the sun. But now she had it every day.

She donned her full, flowered skirt; the white cotton blouse the maid had washed and ironed; and a broad-brimmed yellow straw hat she had bought in the market to keep the sun from her delicate northern skin. She slid her coin purse into the canvas sack she always carried to the mercado and stepped out into the sun.

Sharon Olmstead locked her door and turned. Coming down the concrete stairs into the patio she saw the other Ameri-

can who rented a room there, the stuck-up man who lived on
the roof. He carried a notebook under his arm and wound his
way through the patio overgrown with poinsettias, avocado trees,
jasmine, and ferns. When he saw her he paused, nodded, and
said, "Good morning," but that's all he ever said.

She smiled and said nothing, and he motioned for her to
pass in front of him. She had no choice but to squeeze by the
man and cross the patio ahead of him, stepping on the purple
jacaranda petals that had fallen to earth. As she moved toward
the door that opened onto the street, she could sense his eyes
on her, and her walk felt suddenly awkward. It took forever to
reach the door as she imagined him smirking behind her.

He was probably as old as she, but just the other day she
had seen him taking a young woman to his room in the middle
of the afternoon—some Mexican whore. Sharon had been sitting in the patio in the shade of the jacaranda tree when they
passed by. She pretended to read but could not concentrate on
the words, knowing what they were doing up there. It was all
right for a man to do such things. Men were praised and admired for doing such things. But let a woman do the same and
listen to them laugh. Listen to the laughter.

When he pulled open the heavy wooden door to the street,
Sharon Olmstead stepped onto the stone banqueta and stopped
to look into her coin purse as if she had forgotten something.
He went on before her down the hill toward the center of town.
She waited a few seconds and followed at a distance, finally free
of his gaze.

A block before they reached the zócalo she saw him turn and
enter the Café Cristóbal Colón, and she crossed to the sidewalk
on the opposite side of the street before passing the cafe's open
doors. She held her eyes straight ahead, knowing that Marcos
Celorio would be inside with his friends and that when they saw

her they would all smile their crooked, mocking smiles. She felt herself color thinking of what he must have told them.

At the zócalo she passed before the group of older American men in tennis shorts who met there on the metal park bench every morning. She heard them laugh and turned to cast them a fierce gaze, but they seemed to pay her no attention. She was still a young woman, barely forty, with a very nice face, she had been told. Yet not even the retired men would look at her. No doubt they were like that man upstairs. All they wanted were filthy Mexican girls in order to do filthy things.

Once past the zócalo she turned onto the street that ran to the market, and at the next corner stepped into the Farmacia Así Es La Vida. Her Spanish was sufficient to know what that meant. Mexican humor, she supposed, to name a pharmacy "That's Life," as though sickness and chancres and vile devices were the natural state of creation. Better to live cleanly and die quickly, she told herself.

The young woman behind the counter, the pharmacist's daughter, said to her:

"Buenos dias, señora."

Sharon Olmstead returned a thin, brief smile. Señora. They always said "señora," never "señorita," and she saw that the whole town knew what she had done with Marcos, had seen her dancing with him and going to his house in the middle of the day. They all knew, and behind her back they talked about it and laughed at her foolishness.

She looked straight at the girl and told her what she wanted. The young woman stared back but, under Sharon Olmstead's stern gaze, said nothing. Sharon knew about medicine and pills. Oh, did she know. And she had learned that in Mexico prescriptions were rarely required. So she stared defiantly at the clerk and waited for her order to be filled.

With her pills securely in her sack, she moved on toward the mercado. But today she passed by the stalls of fruits and vegetables without stopping and instead entered the church of Our Lady of Guadalupe, situated just beyond the market.

Inside the church she knelt and looked at the altar with its crucifix and bleeding life-sized Christ, the Resurrected One. She thought of her father and the glory of his resurrection and nearly sneered at the Savior.

She prayed first to the Virgin Mary. It was a long, meandering prayer in which Sharon Olmstead asked for the understanding that she knew only the Virgin could provide and for forgiveness for the sins she had committed—and for those yet to come.

Then she prayed to God the Father. But this was not a prayer of contrition. Rather, she defied God to damn her.

"Damn my father, if you will, if you want to damn someone today. Or damn my brothers who abandoned him to me. Damn the lying gigolo Marcos Celorio Villareal, who coaxed me to dance like a fool and kiss his sex. Damn the arrogant American who takes his Mexican whores upstairs in the afternoon, and damn all the men who laugh behind your back. Damn them all."

Finished praying, she took up her sack and moved back outside. Sharon retraced her steps past the market and the pharmacy, moved through the zócalo, and strode by the Café Cristóbal Colón, where she risked a glance inside and saw her neighbor, the American whoremonger, at a table scribbling away in his notebook. So entranced with himself and his own words and thoughts, never having time for anyone else. Me, me, me.

At the top of the hill, Sharon Olmstead pulled the cord to unlatch the heavy wooden door and stepped from the bright sun of the street into the shaded patio of her home. The patrona, Señora Pola, was there with the maid, Taide, watering the plants and trees. As Sharon approached, Señora Pola turned to her, holding out her hand. In it was a pale purple petal of a jacaranda flower that had fallen from the tree outside her door.

"Que pálida, que delicada, que triste. Aun, siempre el árbol crece más flores, más flores."

Sharon smiled as though she understood perfectly what had been said to her and passed quickly to her room. She had never felt so stupid in her life as she did in Mexico. The Mexicans treated her as a child when they found out she did not understand, using sign language and speaking so slowly—as though she were deaf and stupid. She wanted never again to hear another word of Spanish.

Once in her room she closed the door and pulled the shutters tight against the sun. She took the plastic container of pills from the canvas sack and set it on the crude table that served as a desk, next to the thick tumbler and pitcher of boiled water that Taide brought every afternoon.

Sharon Olmstead counted out twenty-five pills. She had sense enough not to botch the job as her father had and only cripple herself. She shook her head at the memory—the sudden death of her mother, her father's despair, the sound of a gunshot in the middle of the night. And she, the youngest, the girl, was elected to care for the invalid. Who would not live six months, the doctors promised, but who lasted twenty-five years.

And what had she got from it, from her "good works"? The kindness of priests and old ladies, and barely enough to survive on, even in Mexico.

But now there was no going back and nothing to return to but "family." How she hated the word. Brothers who would only smile with satisfaction at her return, at her failure, but who would never help her. *They* would not get a dime of her money. That Marcos had not gotten a dime either, though he tried. All of it would go to the sisters where they first put her after it happened, the only time in her life when there had been no men.

She heard Señora Pola and Taide outside, talking away incomprehensibly, and laughing. Sharon Olmstead poured the tumbler full of boiled water and swallowed down, one by one, the twenty-five pills she had counted out, one for each year. Then she lay on the bed.

It was dark in the room except for lines of sunlight visible around the edges of the shutters. Outside, a breeze passed through the garden.

Chapter

TWELVE

It was late afternoon, and Jake was in his hammock on the terrace outside his room reading his way out of the siesta he'd just woken from.

He had dreamed of her again, something he hadn't done in a long time but that he had done a few times since he had started in with Marta. Although Marta was Mexican and the other was not, Marta nonetheless reminded him of her. There were some similarities in appearance, but also something more than that. Something much more, which was causing him to dream of her.

"Señor. Señor . . ."

He turned to see the head of the maid, who had come halfway up the stairs to call him.

"Sí, Taide."

"Perdóname, but the señora wishes to speak with you."

Jake gestured, holding his thumb and forefinger nearly together. "Momentito."

Taide disappeared, and Jake swung his feet down from the hammock to the stone floor and padded inside for his shoes, wondering why Señora Pola wanted to talk to him. He'd paid his rent on time. Sure, he'd been having Marta up to his room, but Señora Pola had made it clear when he had first taken the place that he was free to use it as he wished. "Libertad completa," she had said.

She was waiting for him in the shade of a lime tree at the bottom of the stairs, leaning on her cane and wearing a worried look on her face. Taide stood behind her with the same expression. Jake said:

"Buenas tardes, señora."

She smiled for an instant to return his greeting then resumed the worried look.

"I am sorry to bother you, but I need your help. We have not seen Señora Olmstead, the gringa who rents the room in back, since yesterday morning. We have knocked and called to her, but she does not answer."

"Are you sure she is inside?"

"She is there. Both the door and shutters are bolted. Perhaps if one could say something to her in English, she would respond."

Jake did not think so and had a bad feeling. He could see from his landlady's face that she wasn't optimistic either.

Jake followed Taide across the flower-strewn patio through the crush of ferns, jacaranda, azucenas, and jasmine. Overhead lay a canopy of palm, avocado, and papaya. Señora Pola moved slowly behind Jake and Taide, using her cane.

They stopped in front of a faded blue door at the far end of the patio, next to a high white wall covered with vines, shrubs, and undisciplined bougainvillea. Jake knocked twice and placed his ear to the door.

"Miss Olmstead. Miss Olmstead."

There was no reply. Jake turned to Señora Pola and whispered: "Qué es su nombre de pila?"

She frowned, then remembered. "Sharón," she whispered back, putting the emphasis on the second syllable.

Jake turned back to the door. "Sharon, are you all right? Is there anything we can do for you? Do you need a doctor?"

A green-backed woodpecker drilled at a tall pine growing on the opposite side of the white wall. Jake looked at Taide and then at Señora Pola, but no one said a word. He turned back to Taide.

"Hay llave?"

She took a key from her apron pocket and handed it to him. Jake put it in the lock, turned it, and pushed on the door. But it didn't budge. He moved to his left and tried the shutters. They shook but would not open. He turned again to Taide.

"Is there something I can use to break open the shutters?"

She moved away without speaking. His eyes met Señora Pola's, and the bad feeling came back.

Taide returned with a short crowbar that he managed to wedge between the wooden shutters. Jake pulled on the iron bar, and the shutters creaked. Then he heard a noise like the breaking of a metal spring, and the left shutter swung open and banged against the wall. And there inside, lying motionless on the bed, he could see her staring back at him.

It was like looking at a diorama of a neatly arranged tableau of death. Sharon Olmstead wore a dark, flowered skirt and a pressed white blouse. She had taken off her shoes, which sat parallel on the stone floor beneath the bed. On the desk at the right was half a glass of water and a pill bottle with the lid off.

She had forgotten to replace the lid on the pills, but otherwise everything was in order.

The night turned cool and windy, so Jake started a small fire of mesquite branches in the chimenea and lay on his bed sipping a shot of old tequila and reading Chekhov. The wind occasionally blew avocados from the trees in the patio, the fruit thumping on the roof or dropping to the terrace outside his door. When one banged against the door itself, Jake looked up, and there she was, peering at him over the high back of the heavy, black armchair at the desk with a mocking leer on her face.

Her face was white, just as it had been when he found her, and she wore the same white blouse. But the expression was one he had never seen on Sharon Olmstead while she was alive. She had always appeared to Jake a shy, old-maidish sort, with a rigid, emotionless face. But now she wore a sluttish expression, the hard face of a whore, and Jake's breath seemed to catch in his chest.

He closed his eyes against the vision. When he opened them she was gone, and he knew he had spooked himself. In Mexico death seemed always near. Too close. It got to a guy and stimulated his imagination.

"Take it easy, Jake," he told himself and knocked on the wooden nightstand in hopes of finding no more bodies in the near future. But when he looked back, there she was again, turning around in the chair and gazing at him over her shoulder. Again he closed his eyes and shook his head, but she wouldn't go away.

"What do you want?" Jake rasped. But he got no answer and felt a fool for talking to a hallucination as though it were flesh and blood. Then, suddenly, she was gone.

Tequila and imagination, Jake reasoned, nothing more. A passing invention brought on by his discovery of her corpse that afternoon. Yes, it had definitely spooked him. Made him start seeing things.

Jake read a while longer and soon turned off the light.

He woke in the middle of the night with the sensation that she was there, and when he reached over and pressed on the lamp, he saw that she had resumed her position in the black chair.

Jake crossed himself—something he hadn't done in years—and said a brief prayer to chase her away. But she remained where she was, smiling at him lecherously, and Jake decided to sleep with the light on.

It was three o'clock the next afternoon, and Jake was at the Café Cristóbal Colón eating a piece of flan and sipping after-dinner coffee when Marta came in. She went first to the corner table and kissed her uncle Don Pablo Martínez on either cheek, then came to Jake and did the same.

Don Pablo waved a greeting to Jake as though he had not seen him sitting twenty feet away for the past hour. But Jake still felt somehow pleased by the belated greeting. Ever since Don Pablo had got it in his head that Jake had killed Marta's fiancé to save Jordan's mural and to win her love, he had shown Jake a courtesy that bordered on deference.

Jake folded away that morning's *Excelsior* as Marta sat across from him, and when he looked up he saw her staring.

"Qué has hecho?" she asked. "What have you been doing? You seem very tired. Perhaps you were diverting yourself all night with one of the gringa whores."

Jake had not found his night with Sharon Olmstead all that diverting. He said: "I did not sleep well."

"You are worried, guapito. Perhaps you are feeling guilt about something. Confess your sins to Father Rosario, and all will be forgiven."

Jake admired the cavalier attitude Marta and her uncle displayed about his presumed assassination of her fiancé and about transgressions in general: Simply confess your mortal sins to Father Rosario and, if you have the clout of the Martínez family, the priest will find a spiritual out.

Jake shook his head. "I do not think the priest can help. Besides, I feel guilt for nothing."

But as he said it, Jake was pricked by something unexpected. Seemingly it had been there all along and now just surfaced into his consciousness: guilt over the suicide of the ghost woman Sharon Olmstead.

They had lived in the same house for months yet remained strangers. Jake had been correct in his behavior: courteous and aloof. Nothing anyone else could fault him for. But he knew why he had shunned her.

Jake looked across the table at Marta, whose bed he had so readily shared even though some believed it was she who had crushed in Pancho's skull while he relaxed in his bath, in order to free herself from an unwanted betrothal. But Marta was a beautiful and exotic young woman; Sharon Olmstead was not and never had been. She seemed like damaged goods to Jake, and he knew to dodge such people, who usually meant trouble. Still, he felt bad about it. But then he felt bad about a number of things.

"Donde estás?" Marta asked. "You seem far away. What molests you?"

"Nada." Maybe it was that his neighbor's suicide stirred in

him old guilt about the other woman, whom Marta resembled. Or maybe he just had gotten some bad tequila. He said to Marta, "Nada importante."

Marta looked at him and shook her head. "One must not worry about the past, Jaque. What's done is done."

Jake usually avoided spending the night with Marta at her place. She slept on the floor on a mat woven of palm fronds, and the next morning he'd have a stiff back. Also, he normally preferred sleeping alone. But these were special circumstances.

They made love on the petate de palma, her body warm and smooth and dark in the candlelight, and Jake found himself forgetting about his ghosts. It was her skin that drew him to her, he realized. The scent of it and its taut youth, which carried him into the past. More than anything else it was that.

She fell asleep in his arms, but when he awoke in the night, he did not feel her body next to him. He turned and saw her sitting up straight, staring toward the doorway. Jake reached over to lay his hand on her thigh, and she grasped it.

"Mira!" she said.

Jake looked where she was staring but saw nothing.

"Como?"

Marta swallowed and pointed and said: "There. Look. Está Pancho!"

"Calma, Marta. Solamente sueñas."

"No, I am awake. I am not dreaming. There he is. Look!"

Jake sat up and took her in his arms and felt her trembling. "Tranquila."

She squinted into the dark. "He was there, as I found him, all white and dripping with water. He looked at me and moved his lips to speak. But when I could not hear his words, he left."

Jake's shirt lay nearby. He took matches from the pocket and lit the candle on the floor by the bed, filling the room with a yellow glow. He stroked her near-black hair. "It's only your imagination. There's nothing there."

Then he felt her body tense, and Marta grabbed the candle and rose to her knees. She held the flame high, and there in the doorway, on the stone floor, were the wet footprints of a man.

Jake focused his eyes on the dark ground as he walked, Marta clinging to his arm. There were no sidewalks or street lamps on the unpaved calle, and a waxing crescent moon provided barely enough light to see where they were going. Jerry-built homes lined the street—hovels constructed of ovate stones and mud bricks, with roofs of corrugated iron and commandeered road signs. A dog barked in the darkness ahead of him, and Jake stopped dead.

"This is foolishness. It will do no good."

"We must try something."

"Tal cosas son supersticiones. I cannot believe in witches and potions and magic spells."

"Last week did you believe in ghosts?"

Six days had passed since Sharon Olmstead first appeared to Jake in his room—and now reappeared whenever he spent the night there. Thus he had no good response to Marta's question, and she led him forward into the darkness:

"Ven, guapito. Está bien."

The street fed into a path that ran along a fetid creek amid cactuses and stunted madroño trees. Jake saw a light on a rise, and they soon moved toward it.

As they approached he saw that the light came from a bare bulb that hung from a pole inside a low stone wall. They stopped by a wooden door in the wall, and Marta called:

"Señora Amelia . . . Señora!"

A dog barked on the other side of the wall, and the high voice of a woman came to them:

"Quién?"

"Marta Martínez Abregón. I have come with a friend to ask your help."

After a moment the door swung open, and they followed the retreating figure of a short, round woman across a dirt yard and into a rustic and dimly lit kitchen, at the center of which sat a square table with four chairs, all homemade and well worn. The woman, thirtyish, with a pockmarked brown face, nodded toward the chairs, and they sat. As he did, Jake noticed two young children studying him from an open doorway. Señora Amelia went to shoo them away and pulled a curtain across the doorway. Then she joined Jake and Marta at the table.

"I will do what I can to help, Señorita Martínez. I will use all my powers to serve you as I have served your uncle in the past."

Jake pondered what the curandera could have done for Don Pablo, a politician with the power and the means to summon doctors and priests and chiefs of police to tend to his needs. Perhaps a spell to cure his gout. If so, Jake doubted that it did much good. He already knew something of her remedies, and what he knew was not good. Marta looked at Jake then back to Señora Amelia.

"We are being haunted, each by our own ghost. Mine is the spirit of my dead novio, Francisco . . ."

The witch nodded and closed her eyes momentarily to show she knew Pancho's story.

". . . who comes each night from the bath where he was murdered. He moves his lips as if to speak, but I cannot hear what he tells me. And the gentleman"—she touched Jake's hand—"is visited by a gringa who killed herself in the house where he lives and will not let him sleep."

"Have you seen the priest?"

"Sí, but he does not wish to help us. Father Rosario says this is not the work of spirits but of the imagination, that we are being punished by our guilty consciences for our lust. He refuses to help except to pray for us to repent of our carnal sins."

This was news to Jake, that Marta had gone to the priest and that the priest was aware of his carnal sins. Jake had always figured that his carnal sins were his own business. He was unaccustomed to small-town life, where your private affairs—or at least some version of them—were public knowledge.

Señora Amelia turned to Jake.

"And the spirit that comes to you, what does she want?"

Jake raised his hands from the table, palms up. "She comes and stares at me from the chair by the desk but does not speak."

"How does she appear? Is she sad? Is she angry? Como?"

"Her face is the face of a whore. Muy agresiva, muy masculina. But when she was alive, she had seemed very timid. Como una solterona. Like an old maid."

"And has she seen you with Señorita Martínez?"

Jake nodded. "Both alive and dead. She came the other night when we believed we were alone."

Jake listened to his own words with a sense of detachment— as though he were somehow outside the trio at the table, looking on—and with skepticism about the truth of those words. Yet it was all true—at least he knew he was seeing something, hallucination or otherwise—and the witch seemed ready to believe him.

The curandera put a finger to her lips and turned back to Marta.

"Tomorrow I will come to town and meet with others who knew the two when they were alive. Then I will talk to the spirit world. When I have an answer, I will send word."

Jake felt as though he were in a dream. None of it seemed real, yet there he was. The next day the witch would meet with his landlady to discuss the ghost that haunted his room. And at first life in Mexico had seemed so simple.

They walked back down the hill and along the dark creek, and the smell of raw sewage surrounded them. Jake shook his head and said to Marta:

"Clearly we are wasting our time with this curandera. When my friend Guillermo, the taxista, was sick with cancer he went to Señora Amelia, who gave him turpentine to drink."

"Y qué pasó?"

"I burned his turpentine so he would not poison himself."

"And what happened to Guillermo?"

Jake hesitated for a few seconds before answering:

"He died."

They moved on in the dark, and Marta also let a moment pass before she spoke.

"I hope this time, Jaque, you will not be so foolish."

Jake checked in at the Hotel Hidalgo on the zócalo and was given a high-ceilinged, windowless room on the ground floor of the colonial building. When Marta came later to sleep with him, she looked up at the wooden rafters and gazed at the splintered door that could be locked only from the outside.

"It's like a dungeon," she said.

"Sí. Como de la Inquisición."

They lay together in the sole bed, whose narrow mattress felt as if filled with straw. Jake turned off the lamp on the table next to them, and they both lay with eyes open in the dark, listening, waiting. But after a while they drifted into sleep, and Jake dreamt.

He dreamt of flying, of soaring over the Bajío, skirting Mexico City, and floating down the valley of Oaxaca as though he'd borne wings. He overflew jungles and, along the coast, pyramids where jaguars crept silently amid the ruins. Marta appeared in a clearing dressed in jaguar hides, and Jake tilted his wings from side to side as he passed, to signal her.

But then Marta began screaming, and Jake was awake in the Hotel Hidalgo. She was beating on him, slapping his face in the dark. He grabbed her and flipped on the light.

Jake then saw it was not him she struck at, but a black bat. It flitted around the lampshade and passed over them, circling and circling, spiraling up above the bed until it alit at the top of the wall and disappeared beside a ceiling beam.

Marta shuddered and held tight to Jake.

"Madre de Dios, Jaque, what have we done so bad as to be visited by the Devil?"

Now Jake shuddered, too, even though he knew in his heart that it was only a bat.

Jake checked out of the Hotel Hidalgo the next morning and went to the Café Cristóbal Colón for breakfast. There Don Pablo Martínez rose from his table and shook Jake's hand.

"Como estás?"

"Más o menos."

"You seem a little tired, Señor Jake."

"I have not been sleeping well."

Don Pablo shook his head sympathetically. "Qué lástima."

Jake sensed that Don Pablo knew about the visitations from the dead gringa that were keeping him awake. Little occurred in the pueblito that Don Pablo did not know about.

"It will pass," Jake said without enthusiasm.

Jake ate eggs with salsa and drank a pot of black coffee, then returned to his house, where he immediately fell asleep in the hammock on the terrace. A light breeze stirred the palms above him and swayed him gently. Jake drifted in and out of consciousness, aware of the songs of warblers and the cooings of Inca doves. At one point he heard a knock on the downstairs door, then the voices of women wafting to him on the wind. He recognized the voice of Señora Pola, then that of the curandera Señora Amelia, and felt somehow reassured. The forces of good—including even white witches—were being marshaled to counteract the forces of evil that seemed to hold him under siege.

In the late afternoon Jake still lay in the hammock, now reading in Chekhov of unrequited love, when Marta appeared on the terrace. She seemed thin and tired yet somehow spirited. She carried a piece of yellow paper that she handed to him.

"Mira. Señora Amelia calls us. She must have a means of dispelling our ghosts or she would not have sent for us so quickly."

"Está bien," Jake found himself saying, falling into the logic of the world he now inhabited—or that inhabited him. A week earlier he had had no experience or belief in the spirit world. Now it dominated his life. Jake grabbed his shoes and his shirt, and they moved to retrace their steps of the previous night.

But at dusk it was a far different journey. Children played in the dusty street as Jake and Marta followed a garbage truck whose driver used a hammer to clang an iron hanging from the side-view mirror. At the sound, women scooted from behind the makeshift walls of their homes toting pastel plastic sacks, through which Jake could see banana peels, scraps of paper, and coffee grounds. Piebald dogs also followed the truck, sniffing at the sacks and scuffling over debris that fell to earth.

Through the open doors of the rustic walled homes, Jake could see bare-earth patios adorned with magenta bougainvillea creeping over the roofs, spreading jacaranda trees laden with pale purple flowers, and tins of bright red geraniums, verdant ferns, and lilies. The sun was setting soft orange behind saw-toothed black mountains on the horizon. He heard a call and looked up to an avocado tree hanging over the street to spy a vermillion flycatcher, iridescent red with black mask and wings.

When the street gave out they again followed the rank creek but soon left it to climb the hill to the house of Señora Amelia. She had made green tea and poured them each a cup as they again sat at the kitchen table.

"I have visited the homes of both Pancho and the gringa, Señora Olmstead. I have talked with others nearby but found no one else who has been molested by their ghosts. Also, I have meditated on what you told me and consulted the spirits for guidance. All this has confirmed what I first believed: The two ghosts are jealous and searching for love.

"They witness the two of you together making love and cry silently for their broken hearts. And until love is returned, they are condemned to roam the earth in search of it."

"Qué horrible!" Marta said. "It is not fair. Why are we made to suffer when we did no wrong? I had consented to wed Pancho even though I did not love him, and it is not my fault he got himself murdered. And Jaque did not know the silly gringa and did nothing to molest her. Why are we being punished?"

The good witch let her eyes rest heavily on Marta for a moment, then moved them slowly to Jake, and he saw that she, too, believed the rumors that he had murdered Pancho. Maybe she also thought that he had used Sharon Olmstead in some way. Jake stared back at Señora Amelia. His conscience was clear, mostly. But at this point he didn't care what the witch thought. All he wanted was a good night's sleep.

Finally Señora Amelia said: "No matter. Whatever acts caused the restlessness of the spirits are of no consequence now. What's done is done."

Marta frowned. "Then there is nothing we can do to make them leave us alone?"

Señora Amelia raised a finger. "Perhaps there is a solution."

The witch paused, and Jake saw Marta biting her lip. Like Marta, he had no good guesses what the curandera might prescribe. Maybe more turpentine.

"The two spirits' quest for love can be satisfied only in the spirit world. There is nothing that you can offer the ghosts to make them go away, at least while you are alive. However, there is something we can attempt: to bring the two ghosts together. That is, to marry the spirit of the lonely gringa to that of your dead fiancé."

Jake saw Marta nodding. He shook his head imperceptibly.

"To move in the spirit world," the witch went on, "we must employ the forces of that world. Thus, to bring about the marriage of Señora Olmstead to Francisco will require the powers of a priest, in order to summon the blessing of Our Lord."

Marta clasped her hands together, as though praying. "But I have been to Father Rosario, and he will not help. He has much hostility and calls me sinful and says we invent the ghosts only to punish ourselves."

Señora Amelia shrugged. "I can help to summon the ghosts. But once they arrive, a priest is required to wed them."

On the dark walk back to the center of town, Marta appeared solemn and thoughtful, barely speaking a word. Twice Jake started to say something, then caught himself. He knew that if he began to talk about it, what he truly thought of the curandera and her mumbo jumbo would soon arise. And there was no point in getting in an argument over how best to dispel ghosts.

He walked Marta to her uncle's house, where she had decided to sleep until Pancho vacated her casita. At the door Jake finally spoke.

"If you truly want a priest for this ghost wedding, why not ask your uncle?"

She stared at Jake with a blank expression. "What do you mean? My uncle is a businessman, not a priest."

Jake lowered his voice. "We know that Don Pablo is a powerful man. Perhaps Father Rosario owes him a favor."

Marta shook her head. "You do not know Father Rosario, nor Uncle Pablo. Such a thing is not possible."

Jake nodded as though in agreement but thought to himself: qué mexicana. How typical of a Mexican woman to believe in ghosts but not in the real world. To trust in God and the inviolability of priests but not in the power of Don Pablo.

Jake kissed her good night and walked back down the hill to the cantina by the bus station. There he sat by the jukebox, drinking from brown bottles of Victoria beer until the bartender turned off the lights. When he got home, Sharon Olmstead was waiting up for him.

Jake managed to get some sleep on the hammock outside his room in the hours near dawn. Then he showered and shaved and at nine o'clock moved down the flight of concrete stairs to the patio, pausing under the pale purple jacaranda tree outside the room where Sharon Olmstead had slept alone, and died.

He shook his head, thinking of what he would now attempt to do for the dead woman. Those he had left behind up north would think he had gone mad. But he had been even crazier then, in those days. But what's done is done.

Anyway, he had had all night to think about what he needed to do and how he would do it. Do it for the hell of it, Jake, if for no other reason, even if you don't believe in it yourself. And he pushed aside the thought that maybe he did believe in it.

At the Café Cristóbal Colón, Don Pablo Martínez sat at his corner table, sipping coffee and chatting with Chief of Police Muñoz. Like all high officials in town, Muñoz was Don Pablo's man.

Jake took a table near the door where he could watch people passing on the street. Jesús brought coffee. Jake glanced at Don Pablo with Chief Muñoz and thought about how Don Pablo had likely retained control of the Revolutionary Party over the years: with favors, friendships, maybe even blackmail. Jake figured that most people in town probably owed Don Pablo for something.

Muñoz got up and tugged at the belt that carried his holstered revolver. After the police chief donned his beige cap with the shiny black bill and moved out the door into the morning sun, Jake stood and walked to Don Pablo's table. Martínez rose and shook his hand.

"Buenos dias, Señor Jake. Como estás?"

"Tengo un problema. A small problem, but one that I cannot solve alone."

Jake paused. Don Pablo said:

"Siéntese. Jesús! Por favor, más café."

Jake sat with Don Pablo and waited until Jesús had poured coffee for them both and retreated. Then he said:

"I would not ask this of you if it did not also concern your sobrina Marta, and if she had not assured me that for me you have respect."

He wasn't sure that was the proper tack, to remind Don Pablo of Jake's presumed murder of Marta's fiancé, an act for which he had apparently earned the pueblito's high regard. To refer to it even obliquely was crude—unnecessarily coarse and direct in the eyes of a Mexican gentleman of Don Pablo's sensitivities and station. But Jake also figured that being a bit crude and direct was perhaps just the right touch in his role as bludgeoning gringo assassin.

Don Pablo smiled a small, closed-mouth smile that made his pencil-thin mustache lie perfectly horizontal above his fleshy lips. Then he nodded once as if to acknowledge Jake's status, that of a serious man who did whatever was necessary to solve his problems. But Don Pablo didn't seem to like being reminded of it. Jake went on:

"I'm sure you know something of our difficulty, of the jealous spirits that are molesting us and causing your niece to sleep at your house."

"Only what Marta has told me, which is very little."

Certainly he knew more than very little, perhaps even more than Jake himself knew. Jake continued as if that were the case:

"The curandera Señora Amelia has suggested that we might rid ourselves of our ghosts by marrying them to one another. But for this we would need a priest, and Father Rosario is not prepared to help. He says that the ghosts are imaginary, visions created by our minds to punish ourselves.

"But our ghosts are real," Jake heard himself saying. "I

know they exist. And I know we must do something to dispel these spirits. That's why I have come to ask your help, Don Pablo."

Martínez shrugged. "I am flattered, but I don't see how I can help. I am but a poor businessman who moves in the commercial world, not the spiritual."

Jake leaned forward.

"I have come to ask you to persuade Father Rosario to perform the ceremony."

Don Pablo spread his hands to plead how powerless he was in such matters but then thought better of it.

He thought that the gringo was not someone who would swallow a lot of mierda. He looked like a man who was running from something. Perhaps from the law. Perhaps he was connected with the drug lords. Maybe that's why he killed Pancho. Not for Marta, nor for his loco Negro friend, but for the cartel.

Don Pablo Martínez was the most powerful man in the municipality, but he knew his limitations. The narcotraficantes had connections in the capital that made his own provincial power seem insipid by comparison. Fortunately, these drug lords had no interest in his poor pueblito. Best to keep it that way. Why take chances? Don Pablo hated taking chances.

But there was also the matter of Father Rosario. Don Pablo disliked calling in such a large debt for so trivial a matter— ghosts! And he knew that Father Rosario would chafe under any such request. But then again, Father Rosario would always be indebted to him, that is, as long as he wished to remain a priest. So it was all right to lean on him from time to time, just so he didn't lean too hard.

Don Pablo Martínez folded his hands on the table and also leaned forward.

"I will see what I can do," he whispered, thinking that perhaps it was a good idea after all to have the cartel owing him a favor.

It was a simple ceremony performed after dark, first at Marta's casita, then repeated in Jake's room on the roof. Jake and Marta served as witnesses, though Jake doubted that Father Rosario would enter their names and the other facts of the union into church records. But otherwise Father Rosario played his role straight, as far as Jake could tell, blessing the rooms before each ceremony and maintaining a solemn and dignified air. Don Pablo had eyes everywhere.

Señora Amelia was on hand to summon the ghosts, but there was no indication that either Pancho or Sharon Olmstead attended the ceremonies. No one present admitted to seeing them, and neither ghost responded when it was time for them to consent verbally to their marriage.

Jake paid Señora Amelia and gave the priest a donation. Father Rosario bowed silently and went off—perhaps to repent of whatever sin Don Pablo had discovered. When they were finally alone in his room, Jake and Marta looked at one another.

"Well?" said Jake.

Marta shrugged. "Tonight we will find out. I will pray to the Virgin and to Jesus and to my patron saint, and you must do the same."

Jake nodded silently.

"Well then, I shall go."

At the door she turned back to Jake and said, "Vamos a ver. We will see," and Jake sensed that she had perhaps even less faith in the ceremony than he did.

Jake bolted the door and sat in bed with the light on as

though reading, one eye on his book, one on the black chair where Sharon Olmstead sat during her visits.

But after an hour, when she had not shown up, Jake turned off the light and lay down. After another few minutes he flipped on the light again. Still nothing. He turned it off and soon was asleep. He dreamt, not of Pancho or Sharon Olmstead but of the other woman who haunted him.

When Jake woke, the sun was already high, beaming down through cracks in the shutters. He sat up leaning on his elbows, looked to the chair by the desk, and moved his head from side to side. Mexico. The surreal landscape and the superstitious people planted all sorts of possibilities in your brain. Irrational suggestions that argued with your senses and led you to see apparitions: love, murder, ghosts. Now he wondered if he had ever seen Sharon Olmstead's ghost at all, if it had materialized as it had gone, by mere suggestion.

Jake stood, pulled on his jeans, and grabbed the glass tumbler he kept by his bed at night. On the desk by the black chair sat the pitcher of boiled water that Taide placed there each afternoon. But as he reached to refill his glass, his hand froze. For there on the rustic desk lay a pale purple flower of the jacaranda tree.

It lay on the edge of the desk just in front of the black chair. Jake picked it up and turned it in his hand and could not remember its being there when he poured his water the night before.

A knock on the door made him start, and he turned and looked at the door and knew it was Marta come to tell him that Pancho had gone.

THIRTEEN

Ever since Sharon Olmstead had killed herself, Jake Harting had taken to sitting outside her door mornings, in the shade of the purple jacaranda tree, reading, making notes in his diary, and discussing Mexican politics with his landlady, Señora Pola López. It was cooler there than on the upstairs terrace outside his room, and he enjoyed the long, rambling conversations with Señora Pola.

She would sit across from him on the stone bench near the center of the garden, her cane leaning against the bench and her cat, Kiko, lying in her lap. Jake once offered Señora Pola the sling chair he had expropriated from the dead woman, but she refused with a shudder and a nervous wave of the hands. Neither would she enter the room where the Wisconsin woman had committed suicide, but would send in the maid, Taide, or the gardener, Bonifacio, when necessary.

She had Jake put up a notice in Spanish and English on the public bulletin board at the presidencia that a room was available. But the only one to come by and look at it—a woman from California recovering from plastic surgery—became suspicious when Señora Pola refused to accompany her into the room.

Yet Señora Pola was happy to sit outside the room in the garden and give Jake her views.

"Of course he is stealing, just like all our presidents before him," she told Jake. "There is too much money from privatization not to steal. Besides, the money has to go somewhere. Still, he will help Mexico."

"Como?"

"By permitting the gringos to come and violate her."

"I don't understand how that helps."

"Perdóname, but your gringo businessmen, unlike Mexicans, are whoremongers, not rapists. They are willing to pay for the privilege of exploiting Mexico. When the Mexican ruling class does it, the people get nothing."

"But the president stole the election, didn't he?"

She shrugged. "Así es la vida."

Jake was glad the room downstairs remained vacant. The garden had become his own private sanctuary, overrun by untamed flowers, vines, shrubs, and trees: azucenas, poinsettias, geraniums, jasmine, ivy, bougainvillea, lemon, papaya, avocado, and scores of other flora whose names he did not know. Kiko crept through the undergrowth stalking birds, mice, and moths. Occasionally Señora Pola would direct Taide or Bonifacio in watering, digging, and sweeping; occasionally she would stop and sit on the stone bench beneath the jacaranda tree to inform Jake on matters such as where the pope was making a mistake. And sometimes, when Marta would come by during siesta to make love, she and Jake would sit in the patio afterward, sipping coffee. But at most times Jake enjoyed perfect solitude in the garden.

One day as Señora Pola came to sit, she stopped to study the purple petals of a flower on the jacaranda tree and frowned.

"Hay problema?" Jake asked.

"Mira."

Jake set down his book and stood beside her.

"The flowers are tinged with yellow. And they do not fall. They cling to the tree and do not mature."

Jake had not noticed previously, but she was right. The flowers had lost their brilliance, and the usual carpet of petals that Taide swept away daily had ceased to appear.

"What do you think it is?"

The old woman looked up at him with eyes wide and cast a meaningful look at the locked door of the dead woman's room.

The jacaranda flowers clung to the branches of the tree, turned yellow, and died. Although the dead flowers still blocked the sun, Jake moved the sling chair back into the shade of a tall pine that grew on the other side of the garden wall.

After a week, Bonifacio showed up one morning with a tall, good-looking youth carrying an ax. The gardener made a line on the tree trunk with a sharp stone. From his sling chair Jake heard Bonifacio instruct the boy on how to swing the ax and how the tree should fall. Bonifacio moved off, and the youth spit on his hands.

On his third swing the ax head flew off the handle and landed at Jake's feet. Jake stood and returned it to him.

"Mira, joven," he said as the boy stared at the ax handle in his hands. "Turn this way and cut from this side. Then if the head flies off again, it will hit the wall and no one will be hurt."

The boy nodded. But when Jake got back to his chair and turned, he saw that the youth had resumed his original position. After a few more swings, the ax head again flew off in Jake's direction. Jake rose once more and carried the blade back to the boy.

He again explained to him in slow, enunciated Spanish how he might better position himself to fell the tree.

"Entiendes?"

The lad nodded, and Jake realized that the boy had not spoken one word. When he again resumed his original position, Jake moved off to the other side of the patio to find Bonifacio.

The gardener was rummaging through the storage room under the stairs.

"The ax is not good, Bonifacio, and I am afraid the boy will accidentally kill me with it. But he doesn't listen to me. Perhaps if you talked to him . . ."

The gardener raised his hands. "No problem. I will take care of it. My son Roberto does not understand well. When he was a child there was an accident . . ."

Bonifacio used the side of his hand to make a hacking gesture at the back of his neck, like an ax blade striking the base of the brain. Jake nodded.

"He is a handsome boy."

"He has sixteen years but will always be a child."

"Are there other children?"

"Sí. Three daughters, all married; two other sons who are both mechanics and another who does well selling wool tapetes; and two infants in the cemetery."

"You do not seem old enough to have grown children. I'm glad they are all doing well. You and your wife must be pleased."

At that Bonifacio looked away, and Jake saw tears spring to his eyes.

"Lo siento. Is it that she is dead?"

Bonifacio shook his head and spat: "She went with another."

Jake put his hands in his pockets. After a moment he said: "Come, Bonifacio. Help us with this tree."

They drove nails into the top of the ax handle to expand the wood and hold the blade tight. Then, with the three of them taking turns chopping, they managed to fell the tree within a half-hour. Bonifacio brought a saw from the storage room, and they stripped the branches and cut them down for firewood. Roberto stacked the firewood neatly under the eaves by the door of the vacant room.

After the work was done, Roberto went inside with Señora Pola to drink a licuado, and the two men stood staring at the tree trunk. All that remained of the purple flowering tree was a gnarled stump, the ax leaning against it. Bonifacio shook his head.

"I know the señora will want this out. But the roots go deep and they are tough. Much work."

"Dynamite?" Jake suggested.

Bonifacio laughed for a second, then continued frowning at the stump.

"This is the difficult part," he said, "but I will complete it."

Yet for some reason Bonifacio did not return to finish the job. Jake continued sitting in the garden mornings for another week but then gave it up and simply stayed on the terrace outside his room. The tree stump bothered him, though he couldn't say exactly why. He figured it must have bothered Señora Pola as well, for she no longer came to talk.

Every day now, as he descended the concrete stairs from the terrace and moved across the patio to the door that opened onto the street, Jake had to pass the trunk with the rusting ax leaning against it. He wished to hell the gardener would take the damn ax and hack the thing out. There was no point in leaving that ugly stump there. It wasn't as if it would ever grow back. And Jake wondered if Bonifacio, too, wasn't spooked by the dead woman.

Marta and Jake were naked on the narrow bed in his room on the roof; the sheet had been kicked to the floor beside Marta's short black skirt and Jake's jeans. Jake had hold of Marta's wrists, and she pulled him into her rhythmically with her long, brown legs, which she had wrapped around him and hooked with her ankles at the small of his back. He licked her breast, and the muscles in her neck tightened. She muttered through clenched teeth, "Así! Así!" It was then that they heard a key in the door.

Jake stopped and turned halfway as the maid, Taide, came into the room from the terrace, set a pitcher of boiled water on the desk, and pivoted to leave. When she saw them naked together on the bed she said, "Perdón," and exited as though in a trance.

Jake shut his eyes, shook his head, and rolled off Marta.

"Sigue!" Marta said. "Continue!"

"No puedo ahorita. My concentration has been broken."

Marta put the back of her hand to her mouth and smiled. Jake glanced at her and stared at the ceiling with his hands behind his head.

Once a week Taide cleaned Jake's room and each afternoon brought him a pitcher of freshly boiled drinking water. It was not uncommon for Marta to come by during siesta to make love with Jake, but Taide had always avoided coming up to the terrace when she was there.

"What's wrong with that maid?"

"But it was you who were rude to her," Marta said.

"Como?"

"By not inviting her to join us."

Jake sat on the side of the bed and opened one of the beers sweating on the nightstand.

"I don't believe she would accept such an invitation. Señora Pola tells me that Taide has never married, that she is a señorita. And that now she is entering the change of life."

Marta said: "This has happened once before."

Jake turned and looked at her. "Taide had never walked in on us before today."

"Not the maid. La otra. The ghost of the dead woman."

He put a pillow against the white stucco wall and leaned against it. Marta took the beer from Jake and sipped.

"It was the same. We were making love, and we were both very excited. Then you turned and saw her, and stopped."

"I remember."

"But why did you stop, Jaque? I was hot and ready to finish."

"You are always ready."

Through the blue curtain drawn across the open shutters came a breeze and the roar of a Saturday crowd from the bullring in the next street. Jake went on:

"It is different for a man. A man needs to concentrate. To penetrate, one must focus one's thoughts." Jake made a wedge with his two hands held together. "But a woman is always ready to make love. A woman is never satisfied."

"Not when a man quits before she finishes."

"Mira, bonita. I cannot make love with others watching."

"Then you will never make a good Mexican, Jaque. Perhaps you are too Anglo-Saxon."

Jake liked the way it sounded in Spanish: anglosajón, with the "j" pronounced like an "h" and the accent on the last syllable. He liked the way it looked on her lips. He took the beer back from Marta and pulled her on top of him.

"Sí, yo soy muy anglosajón y muy gringo. If they wish to watch me perform, they must pay."

Afterward, Jake sat naked on the bed smoking a cigarette and watching Marta as she slipped into a sleeveless yellow top that did not quite reach her waist. She bent to pick up the short black skirt from the floor and pulled it up over her brown legs, and Jake saw that it clung to her hips and thighs and showed how long her legs were. The black bikini she had worn earlier lay on the chair by the bed. When she picked it up and put it in her purse, Jake asked:

"Porqué no lo llevas? Why don't you wear it?"

Marta came over to kneel on the bed, grabbed Jake's hand, and put it beneath her skirt.

"Because you may wish to make love again, and I want to be ready."

They drank another beer while he dressed, then moved outside and down the concrete stairs to the garden below. As they passed the door of the room where Sharon Olmstead had taken the overdose of sleeping pills, Marta crossed herself.

Jake's eyes fell to the stump of the jacaranda tree opposite her door, the rusted ax still leaning against it. It reminded him of her suicide. He had paid her no mind before. But now that she was dead, he felt her presence more than when she was alive.

As they passed the kitchen of the main house, Marta said, "Jake. Look."

Through the glass-and-wrought-iron doors he saw Taide standing motionless in the middle of the kitchen with a broom in her hand. Marta and Jake passed not ten feet away, but Taide did not seem to notice them. She stared off at nothing, as though seeing a vision, and Marta again crossed herself.

At the Café Cristóbal Colón there was but one empty table, near the door. As Marta and Jake sat, a group of bullfight aficionados at a long table in the back of the restaurant broke into song. When Jake turned back to the street, he saw Jordan passing on the sidewalk. Jordan came over, and they shook hands.

"Glad I saw you," Jordan said. "Got an opening tonight at Efrin's gallery. Come over after you eat and bring your chick. It's my best stuff. A new wave. I think I'll call it my 'big black' period. Anyway, I'm gonna make a killing and pay you back double."

Jordan bowed to Marta, turned on his heel, and went off down the street, hands tucked into the pockets of the black windbreaker he wore in all weather. Marta looked at Jake and touched her forefinger to her temple.

"Pasado."

Jake nodded. "Sí. He is somewhat mad."

"Then why do you have him as a friend?"

Jordan was the only anglosajón in town that Jake had befriended—insofar as a light-skinned Harlem Negro was Anglo-Saxon—although there were a number of other Americans, Brits, and Canadians around who were no doubt more sane and less expensive to have as friends.

"Because he is a mad artist. At times he sees things no one else sees."

Marta nodded as though she understood.

They strolled down the street toward the zócalo, where a full moon sat on the roof of the cathedral in front of a darkening sky.

At the gallery they followed the noise of conversation to the workshop in back, where scores of people milled about, sipping punch from plastic cups. Marta spied two of her aunts and moved off to talk. Jake made his way through the crowd under the veranda, where paintings were hung along the wall.

The canvas roof that covered the patio at the center of the work area had been folded back to the night sky. There a small band—guitar, flute, double bass, bongos—began to play.

He saw Jordan's signature on a series of oversized oils depicting a black penis in progressive stages of erection. "Sold" tags had been taped to two of the frames. In addition there were oil and watercolor nudes by other artists and sugar sculptures of copulating skeletons.

Jake spied Jordan talking with two elderly gringas, and the artist waved him over. As Jake approached, one of the women shook Jordan's hand and told him how thrilling it was to meet a true artist. When the two men were alone, Jordan handed Jake an envelope and said in a low voice:

"Here's five hundred pesos. I'll have the rest tomorrow."

As Jake put the envelope in the back pocket of his jeans, Jordan shook his head.

"I spent all those years being intellectual, trying to paint like Rivera and Orozco." He lifted his chin at his canvases. "This is what I should have been doing all along. This is what people want. You can't expect . . ."

Suddenly Jordan stopped speaking and frowned at something over Jake's shoulder. Jake noticed that the room had quieted except for the smooth salsa coming from the band, and he turned.

There, at the center of the patio, just in front of the band, Marta moved fluidly to the music, head back as though studying the stars, or perhaps the moon, which had just shown itself over the veranda. But then Jake saw that her eyes were closed.

Her hips shifted rhythmically in the short skirt; her palms she held flat against the bare brown skin that showed between the bright yellow blouse and the black skirt. Everyone including the musicians had fixed their eyes on her as if possessed, and no one spoke.

Jake felt a chill run through him, then found himself moving toward her. When he reached Marta he placed his hands on her waist, breathed in her scent, and began to move with her.

Beneath the veranda the two old women who had been speaking to Jordan touched hands and slid their feet back and forth to the salsa. Jordan held his arms outstretched toward the stars and pirouetted under the night sky. Soon everyone was dancing, and the band played on and on.

Marta and Jake moved back across the zócalo and walked without speaking toward her casita, winding over deserted cobbled streets through a maze of high Spanish walls. Jake felt Marta's body brush against his and smelled the perfume in her hair. When he glanced at her, he saw her lips held parted as they walked, her large, Moorish eyes glassed and distant.

They moved up the Calle de San Francisco with the moon ahead of them. At her door he grabbed her bare arm, and she turned to him. Jake pressed her up against the stucco wall and kissed her lips, sliding his hand under her blouse. She moved her hips forward against his and raised her left knee, her short black skirt riding up to show her thigh in moonlight. Jake put his hand there and ran it up the back of her leg. She pulled at his zipper, and in a moment he was in her. He bent and lifted her tight yellow blouse to lick her breast. Marta's eyes rolled back, her breath quickened, and her body quivered.

Behind him on the opposite sidewalk Jake sensed footsteps. The footsteps paused then, after a moment, continued. He saw Marta's eyes focus for an instant on whoever it was, but then she went back to where she had been inside herself, and Jake went with her.

He moved alone back across the square and up the hill toward home.

The night was still clear, the sky rich black with silver stars, the moon like plaster, but the wind now blew. It came across the high plateau from the Pacific, and behind the high walls he could see palms waving and hear their fronds slapping together. A dog bayed somewhere nearby, and to his right a cat ran across the broken glass embedded in mortar atop a wall.

Jake glanced over his shoulder as he walked, feeling someone following him, but there was no one. The wind carried something foreign in it, and Jake hurried up the hill.

When he reached the casa, he again looked behind him as he unlocked the heavy wooden door and stepped into the courtyard. Jake strode across the junglelike patio and past the mutilated jacaranda tree but then looked up and stopped before he reached the concrete stairs, his heart rising in his chest.

For poised on the corner of the flat roof at the top of the stairs was the maid, Taide. She wore a white nightshirt that hung to her feet; she faced the moon, hands folded over her heart. Her long black braid had been undone, her tresses and the nightshirt waving in the night wind. The moon shone on her face, and she stood silhouetted against the black sky behind her.

Jake moved slowly up the stairs and saw that she stood balanced on the narrow wall that guarded the rear of the patio. He called softly to her:

"Taide. Taide."

After a few seconds she turned and whispered: "Está cerca."

Jake rasped: "What is near? Who is near?"

She turned away, and Jake looked down and stood frozen on the stairs. For he saw that she was dancing, that her feet were moving ever so slightly back and forth across the shards of broken glass cemented into the top of the wall, and the blood from her ribboned feet crept down the white wall like purple flowers flowing into the earth.

"Taide!" he whispered. "Come to me."

At his words her eyes rolled back into her head. He grabbed for her, and she collapsed into his grasp.

Jake lifted her in his arms to carry her down the stairs to her room and was surprised at how light she felt, as though the woman were more spirit than flesh.

FOURTEEN

Chief of Police Hector Muñoz Pineda tossed his black-billed cap on the table by the front door, hung his belt with the hand-cuffs and holstered revolver on the hook on the wall, and patted the paunch that was beginning to grow over his belt.

"Soy yo," he called toward the kitchen, where he heard women's voices and the clatter of plates.

He received no answer.

Muñoz moved to the dining room, where he found Josefina, their servant, clearing away dishes from the after-noon meal.

"Buenas tardes, señor."

He looked at the emptied table and raised his hands.

"Qué pasa?"

Josefina said only: "There is a plate for you in the kitchen. I will bring it now."

One by one his two youngest daughters came from the kitchen and kissed his cheek.

"Hola, Papa," said the youngest. "We have to return to school now to rehearse for the Christmas program."

"Christmas? Already?"

"Sí," was all she said and soon was out the door with her sister, moving past the hanging revolver that was out of her reach just yesterday, and Muñoz shook his head at the passing of his life.

When he turned back, his wife stood in the doorway of the kitchen with a plate in her hands.

"Siéntese."

Muñoz looked at her for a moment before deciding not to say anything and took his chair at the end of the table as ordered.

Josefina brought hot tortillas, and his wife stood over him as he ate. After a minute of silence, she said:

"We waited. The girls had rehearsal. So we decided to eat."

Muñoz looked up from his chicken and rice and opened his mouth to ask his wife if she, too, was in the school Christmas program, but caught himself. He rolled a piece of chicken inside a tortilla and chewed in silence. After another minute she said:

"Did you speak to Don Pablo about Christmas dinner?"

"Why is everyone talking Christmas? It's barely November. And what is this about dinner with Don Pablo?"

"You don't remember? We talked about inviting him for Christmas dinner. Now is the time to ask."

She was always referring to conversations of which he had no recollection, and he wondered if maybe he was growing old too fast. Tequila would do that to a man, it was said. Muñoz answered as he chewed.

"But if I invite him now, when he has yet to receive any other invitations, he might accept. And I have no wish to spend a holy day with a son of a bitch."

There was a third silence, and Muñoz called toward the kitchen:

"Josefina! Una cerveza, por favor."

Josefina brought him a beer in a brown bottle while his wife looked on. When the servant had retreated to the kitchen, Señora Muñoz said:

"If not for Don Pablo you would not be chief of police. His family and mine have always shared responsibility for the pueblito, ever since colonial times. It would not harm you to acknowledge that and show him respect."

"I show him respect every day by kissing his behind three times, morning, noon, and night. I think that should be sufficient."

She shook her head. "Sin respeto."

"Yes, I am an ugly American," he said in English. "I have no respect for conquistadors and thieves."

"Mande? What did you say?"

"Nada. Nada," he said, but he knew that was at the core of the running argument with his wife, a discussion that had now lasted some thirty years. He was not fully Mexican, but Mexican American. A dual citizen. And although he had spent most of his fifty-odd years in Mexico, the gringos had tainted him, in her eyes. Vulgar and disrespectful of sacred institutions: the Church, the family, and the system of classes that kept Josefina in the kitchen and kept Don Pablo fat and comfortable. Yes, America had ruined him.

"Will you speak to Don Pablo . . ."

"Chinga Don Pablo," he muttered to himself as he chewed.

". . . before you leave for your 'conference'?"

So that was it. That was the reason behind the dinner alone and the cross-examination. Muñoz set down his fork and stared at the handcuffs on the wall in the next room. "Esposas," the Mexicans called them: Wives.

"What do you mean by that?"

"By what?"

"By the way you said 'conference,' as though you were questioning my integrity—as though my work was any business of yours."

"I do not question your 'integrity.' We already know of what that consists. Nor do I wish to interfere in your work. But when you tell me you are going to Monterrey for a police conference when in fact you are visiting your whore in Texas, that concerns the family, which is my province."

Some day, he thought, I will take the gun from the wall and shoot one of us. I will end this conversation.

"Listen to me now, my dearest little sweet potato. I will say this once, and then we will speak no more of it. I am traveling to Monterrey for the annual conference of provincial chiefs of police, where I will spend a week discussing jails and laws and drug enforcement. I swear on the head of my mother and the body of Christ that this is so. If you choose not to believe me and instead to imagine unpleasant things, I cannot prevent you. Now I will eat my comida in peace."

Muñoz once again picked up the tortilla and the fork and bent over his dinner, wondering how she always managed to figure out what he was up to, even when he himself wasn't sure what he was doing. She saw into the future and the past and across borders into foreign lands, as well as colors of the spectrum that normal humans could not view. She was a witch. But gracias a Dios, she had not yet divined that the "whore" in Texas was also his wife.

Muñoz woke at five a.m. and carried his bag to the car while the household slept. The drive to the border was long and boring, and he would not arrive at Laredo until after dark. Yet he relished the quiet hours alone on the road that led to the land of his birth.

He put the bag in the trunk of the Ford with Texas plates, unlocked the metal doors that closed the wall surrounding his home, and was soon on the dark highway. Muñoz rolled down the window to allow the cool, high-desert air to blow against his face and let out a long breath that he seemed to have been holding for months.

He loved Mexico—la chingadera—and Mexicans and the rawness of the land. His land, his people. But it was always the same when he left for the border. He felt as though he were traveling into a future where there was hope.

He remembered now the first time he had felt it. He was seventeen and without work and had been ordered to report for duty in the army of the Estados Unidos de México. Instead, he crossed the border at Matamoros with three words of English—"I am American"—and handed over the papers that showed he had been born to migrant farmworkers at Nacogdoches, Texas.

He continued to feel hopeful when ordered to report for duty in the army of the United States of America. He shot his rifle better than anyone else, and even though he could not speak English and had no idea what his new country was fighting for, they gave him a marksmanship ribbon and sent him on a ship to Vietnam. There he sat in a tree with his rifle, not knowing if he was Mexican or American or Chinese, and shooting everything that moved regardless of nationality.

Hector Muñoz Pineda smiled at the memory as a red sliver of sun peered over the black mountains on his right. He saw himself sitting alone in a tree in a strange land, not knowing who he was or where he belonged but never relinquishing hope, clinging to his rifle and to the certainty that things had to get better.

He pulled the Ford to the curb at a schoolyard where both Hispanic and towheaded children ran, seesawed, and jumped rope. Muñoz turned to rub the head of Hector Junior and to receive a kiss from Silvia before they sprinted from the car with their books to join the others.

"Pasando la vida. How long now, Patricia, have we been together?"

The woman next to him counted on her fingers. ". . . diez, once, doce. Twelve years in January."

He looked from the playground to her. She was still a young woman, barely thirty-five, and the short-cropped hair made her look even younger.

"Twelve years? No. Then you must have been nine when I first seduced you. You seem so young, so pretty."

She shook her head at him and sucked her teeth as though she disapproved of such talk, but he could see she was pleased by the compliment.

"If you are so impressed by my youth and my beauty, then you will of course treat me to a holiday."

"Claro. Whatever you wish."

She slid over next to him and grabbed his arm. "Let's go for a ride—like we used to back home. I seldom see the campo anymore."

"Do you mean to see the campo or to make love in my car again?"

She shook a finger at him. "I am a married woman now. Do not suggest such things."

"Yes, you are. And the mother of my children."

She kissed his cheek and said:

"Life is beyond our imaginations. We could never have invented all that has passed."

"Nunca."

She was right. He would have never guessed he could fall in love at that age with a woman almost as young as his oldest daughter. Nor that she would get pregnant. Nor that his wife would discover that fact. It was then he took Patricia to the United States and married her so she could legally remain and there bear his child. Hector, his only son, and Silvia had been born in Laredo and spoke English well enough to teach their mother. Americans, one hundred percent.

"Perhaps we could go to Eagle Pass."

"Perhaps we could go somewhere closer. Eagle Pass is a hundred miles away, and my ass is sore from driving all day yesterday."

She kissed him again.

"Please, Hector. You can drive as fast as you want, and I promise I will not complain, and we will be there in an hour and a half."

"Not if we stop to make love every ten miles as we once did."

"Sí, mi guapo. Then we would not arrive until Christmas."

She said it in English, and she said it very well, and Muñoz could not say no to his American wife.

The closer they got to Eagle Pass, the quieter she became. At Carrizo Springs she began tearing at a handkerchief she held in her lap, and Muñoz pulled the car to the shoulder of the road.

"Estás preocupada. Qué te molesta? What is it, Patricia?"

She looked at the handkerchief and shrugged. He waited in silence. Finally she said:

"My cousin Guadalupe is at Piedras Negras with her baby. She wants to see a doctor."

Hector Muñoz looked at his wife for a moment, thinking. Then he said:

"You mean she wants to come to the States for treatment." Patricia nodded.

"How?"

"They will be near Eagle Pass at noon, and she will come across the river on a raft."

Muñoz shook his head. One wife was understandable. Any man can make a mistake. But two wives, that was the work of a true jackass. He said:

"You know that when I was a coyote they put me in jail at El Paso for two weeks. Next time I'm caught running wetbacks, I pay $600 and spend six months in jail. How would that look, for the chief of police to be sitting in jail?"

"She is ill."

"Then we can take her to a doctor in Mexico. I will pay for her visit. But I cannot risk bringing her in. No. I am sorry. Now show me where she will come across so we can send her back."

Muñoz started the engine, and neither husband nor wife said a word until she told him where to turn off the highway.

It was hot as hell for November, and there was little shade on the bank of the Rio Grande. Muñoz stood with hands on hips shaking his head. A raft, she had said. On the other side he saw two coyotes positioning Patricia's cousin in an inflated inner tube, her infant in her arms. Fucking Mexicans. She wore a faded, sky blue cotton dress and carried a plastic sack with her belongings. Again he shook his head.

One of the men signaled to Muñoz and bent to grab a rope that lay on the bank. The rope looped around the trunk of a willow tree on the American shore, ran back across the river bottom, and circled a tree trunk on the Mexican side. Muñoz pulled, and the men on the far side did the same. Patricia stepped beside him and fit her hands to the rope as well. They pulled together, and the gray inner tube holding the woman and the child began to move across the waters.

Muñoz thought, Patricia was right. Life is beyond our imagination. He watched her strain against the rope and felt how strong she was. She was lean and hard and wiry, with a toughness that came from the arid campo where she was bred. She was all his wife—his other wife—was not. And though he called Patricia his American wife, she was just as Mexican as the other, and perhaps more so.

The inner tube, now shiny black with water, bounced across the brown river, and he saw the cousin, Guadalupe, clinging to her child. It was no doubt the same with her as it was with him whenever he crossed the border: America was hope, Mexico resignation. But as the tube neared the American shore, Muñoz braced himself for what he now had to do. Guadalupe's hope would be short-lived. Back to Mexico, back to being resigned to hard fate. It was shit, but he had to do it.

The rubber raft scraped against the rocky shore. Patricia waded ankle deep into the water and bent to take the infant from her cousin's arms. Muñoz extended a hand toward Guadalupe, and she gave him a smile that reminded him of

Patricia's. They grasped arms, and Muñoz leaned forward to pull her soaking from the raft. He saw where the water had pressed the thin dress to her breasts and noticed that her left breast was bleeding.

He pulled her to her feet, and she hugged Patricia. Muñoz turned away as he heard his wife saying to her:

"Lupe, hay un problema. No es posible . . ."

He did not want to look at the woman. No, we cannot imagine life, cannot imagine how hard it will be. We look to the future with hope, seeing only happiness, never the hard truth. Easy delusion, hard truth. Cousins to hope and resignation. He turned back and said:

"Mira . . . No es posible—hoy. Today is not good. One has not prepared. Pero, . . . mañana. Tal vez mañana. One must see how the gringos move and where are their checkpoints. Go back across to your coyotes, cousin. Tell them: tomorrow, in the morning. And today I will prepare."

They lowered Guadalupe back into the inner tube and handed her her child.

When Muñoz and Patricia were once again in the Ford where Hector Junior had been conceived, she reached across and took his hand.

"I will go to the church and pray and ask the saints and the Virgin and the Lord to protect us. And know that come what may, I will always remain true. Come the worst, I will visit you every day."

"Gracias. Muchas gracias. Thank you so much for the comforting words." He started the engine of the Ford. Once again up a tree, he thought, not knowing where he would land.

The next morning Patricia took Hector Junior and Silvia to her neighbor while her husband still slept. But when she returned, he was leaning against the kitchen counter drinking coffee.

"Donde están los niños?" he asked.

"I took them next door, so Carmela can care for them today. It is a school holiday."

"Which?"

"Veteran's Day," she said in English.

"Good. Then maybe all the border patrols and immigration cabrones will be off getting drunk, and we will have no problems." But he knew there could very well be problems.

After they had sent Guadalupe back across the Rio Grande the previous day, they spent the afternoon clocking the border patrols and studying the checkpoints. It was not so good. But the Ford had Texas plates, and if the gringos saw just the two of them in the front seat with the baby, everything would be okay. Maybe. He hoped. There was another cousin in San Antonio, and a cancer clinic, and once they got Guadalupe away from the border it was done. They would be back in Laredo that night. God willing. Ojalá!

The drive to Eagle Pass seemed to take forever, and when they got there it appeared that the town had been overrun by state police and the military. Squad cars were parked along the curbs, and uniformed soldiers congregated on street corners.

"Something is up," he said to Patricia. "I do not like this."

"Qué pasa?"

"I do not know. Maybe drugs. Maybe wetbacks. Please, Patricia, say another prayer."

They took U.S. 277 north toward Quemado but turned left onto a dirt road before they reached town. They followed the rutted road to the river, and the coyotes were again waiting by their pickup truck, along with Guadalupe in her blue dress.

Once again the men lowered Lupe into the inner tube and handed her the child. She placed the sack with her possessions on her lap. Once again Muñoz and Patricia grabbed the rope and pulled, and the coyotes pulled on the other side of the loop and fed the slack back toward the raft.

Soon she was across, and Patricia took the infant Pedro from her arms. Muñoz made Guadalupe lie on the floor in the back of the car, under a blanket. He lit a cigarette, then turned and waved to the men on the far side of the river. They waved back. Muñoz took two puffs on the cigarette and threw it to the ground.

After ten minutes on the highway, Muñoz realized something was wrong, and he lit another cigarette.

"No hay tráfico. Not one car has passed going the other way. Perhaps the gringos are making a special operation. A roadblock. A checkpoint."

"Should we turn around then and go the other way, toward Del Rio?"

"I do not know. Madre de Dios! Women, pray for us."

U.S. 277 ran downriver toward Eagle Pass. Muñoz kept his eyes on the road ahead, and no one said a word. As they reached the city limits, he slowed the gray sedan and ahead saw a line of cars stopped on the highway in front of him. When Patricia saw it, she gasped.

Muñoz knew enough not to slow down prematurely or try to turn around or do anything that might draw the attention of the gringo bastards. They may be looking only for drugs with their dogs. And he had his American passport and Texas plates, for whatever those were worth.

"Chinga los gringos!"

Pedro began to cry, as though he, too, sensed trouble. Patricia crossed herself, kissed the infant, and began praying aloud in Spanish. Muñoz rolled his eyes.

"Please, woman, try not to act so Mexican."

He pulled the Ford to a stop behind a semi at the end of the line of vehicles and waited. After five minutes the line had not moved. Muñoz smoked and tried leaning out the window to see around the truck, but it was too wide. And he did not want to step out into the street and draw attention to himself. So he rested his arm on the steering wheel, stared at the back of the truck, and thought of his colleagues at the provincial chiefs of police conference in Monterrey. After another minute he said:

"Remember, Patricia, you promised to visit me in the can every day."

She turned to him red-eyed, with lips pursed together, and he shook his head and looked away.

It was then he heard the music. At first he thought it was a radio, but then he heard the drums. Muñoz opened the car door and stepped out. He looked past the truck and began walking forward toward the sound.

At the head of the line of cars he stepped to the curb of a cross street and stood behind a group of children as a high school band passed lockstep. Then came teenage girls in sequined suits, twirling batons.

Muñoz now noticed the red-white-and-blue bunting tied to the light poles of Eagle Pass, when before he had noticed only the police and military. He lifted his hands and applauded. He applauded the band and the majorettes and his own good luck. Do not give up hope yet, you hopeless Mexican bastard. You are not in jail yet. And you are not yet dead.

A man his own age came marching down the street carrying an American flag and behind him two older men holding up between them the blue-and-gold banner of the Eagle Pass Veterans of Foreign Wars.

Muñoz pushed past the children in front of him, stepping into the street. The parade of old soldiers passed, and Muñoz stood alone, at attention, saluting.

Border patrols overtook them twice as they headed east on U.S. 57. Patricia prayed out loud as the cars pulled next to them, and Muñoz prayed silently that he would not foul his pants. But neither patrol pulled them over.

They picked up Interstate 35 north of Pearsall and stopped at a rest area twenty miles down the highway, on the outskirts of San Antonio. It was done.

When Muñoz came out of the men's room, he saw Patricia and Guadalupe kneeling side by side, praying aloud in Spanish, giving thanks to the hand of God that had guided and protected them. Little Pedro lay on the ground beside them, squirming and kicking on the blanket that had covered his mother on the floor of the car.

Muñoz passed two young Anglo couples at a picnic table and saw them looking at his wife and her cousin, and laughing. He heard one of the men say:

"They're praying they won't have to pick any more tomatoes."

Muñoz stopped and turned. He stared at them, and the couples looked away. He opened his mouth to speak, then hesitated. He started again to say something and stopped. He turned his back to them and walked past his wife to the car.

Chapter

FIFTEEN

Jake climbed the narrow goat path up the side of the arroyo by the waterfall. Its spray made a rainbow in the gorge beneath him that seemed to soften the hard earth. He moved up and up, eyes focused on the ground where cactus flowers bloomed amid a scrub of mesquite and sage. It was nothing like the summertime tangle of growth he had known up north, but rather rocks, sand, and spiny cactus, with black mountains on the horizon reminding him how far he was from home. No fences, as though the land wasn't worth the effort.

He came to the shelf that ringed the arroyo and, as he pulled himself up, saw the pueblito on the horizon, the place where he had settled for now. The clean, hard earth seemed right for now. Jake saw the spire of the cathedral in the distance, and the mountains and the blue sky, and he took a deep breath.

"Señor . . ."

Jake turned. A goatherd perched on a boulder in the shade of a stunted elm tree shifted his machete to his left hand and touched the brim of his soiled straw sombrero.

"Good day, lord."

Jake saluted. "Buenos dias."

He offered Jake water from a leather bota slung over his shoulder. Jake moved into the shade with the goatherd, lifted his baseball cap, and wiped perspiration from his forehead.

"No, gracias."

Water sounded good, but the campesino likely filled his goatskin from the stream that fed the waterfall, and Jake's stomach was not acclimated to the groundwater. Even Cortéz and his conquistadors had complained about the water, Jake knew, so he did not feel unmanly about refusing.

"De donde es usted?"

"De los Estados Unidos, but now I live there, in the pueblito."

The goatherd looked at the steeple in the distance then back to Jake. "Tienes pistola?"

Before he knew Jake was a gringo, the goatherd had called him "lord." Now he had lapsed into the familiar form. Jake shook his head.

"No tengo pistola."

The man stroked his hoary chin as he squatted in front of Jake. "With a pistol I could kill the rattlesnakes and the vultures, and have rabbits to eat. If you could bring a pistol and some bullets, I would share the meat with you."

Jake had never thought about rattlesnakes before, but now knew he would whenever in the campo.

"Your offer is generous. I will consider it."

"If you return and I am not here, you can place the pistol in a plastic sack and leave it between these two rocks."

Jake returned his cap to his head and touched the bill, and the goatherd did likewise.

He found a path that headed off toward the pueblito and followed it.

The path passed a small village Jake had not seen before. Pigs rooted in the bare earth surrounding five mud-brick homes, and the smell of them came to him on the wind. He followed the path down into a gully and at the bottom found shattered bottles and rusted cans, along with broken bricks and shreds of paper and cloth. Then he saw clean-picked bones lying on the earth and plastic sacks of rotting garbage, and he again held his breath.

The path rose, and as he reached the top of a small hill he stopped. Jake stood before a field of short cactuses. Clinging to the spines of each pad of every plant were plastic sacks, the pastel bolsas that were the Mexican national packaging, handed over by shopkeepers with every five-cent purchase. The sacks flapped and snapped in the wind, and it was as though they were growing there, as if Mexican scientists had somehow perfected a hybrid nopal whose fruit could be used to carry home the Coca-Cola. All that was missing was a crew of campesinos harvesting them.

After the path left the garbage dump the walk got better, but it seemed to take a long time to reach town, and when he got there he was thirstier than ever.

On the dusty plaza where the buses stopped for passengers sat a cantina Jake liked because it was always cool and usually empty, and he stepped in from the sunshine to the unlighted bar.

Ceiling fans turned lazily above the bartender, who chatted to a lone customer at the other end of the bar. Jake moved to the rail and when the barman came toward him, called for a beer to clear the dust from his throat.

As his eyes adjusted to the dim light, Jake saw the other man at the bar motioning him over and realized it was Marcos. Jake grabbed his beer as it was placed in front of him, cursed silently, and moved down the bar.

Jake knew Marcos from the Café Cristóbal Colón and had seen him about town, usually with some gringa or other. Like many other young men in the pueblito, Marcos seemed to live off the wind—except he wasn't as young as some. He was always about town with money in his pocket, but Jake had no guess how he got it. Import-export. Drugs. Family.

"Buenas tardes," said Jake.

"What's happening?" Marcos responded in English, and the bartender turned away and stared out the door to the street. The two men shook hands. Marcos smirked and said:

"I've seen you around town with Marta Martínez lately. A beautiful girl."

Jake didn't like the way he said it but decided to ignore that. "Yes, she is."

"But I have always thought your American women more interesting in bed than Mexicans. More free. Eh?"

This was what Jake had been trying to put his finger on, what it was about Marcos that repelled him: He was oily and sexually unsettled, as if he were still struggling through puberty. Jake just shrugged. Marcos raised an eyebrow.

"A very beautiful girl, Marta. You are a lucky man."

Jake wanted to change the subject and just then noticed a pale green plastic sack on the floor at the bar rail, partially hidden by Marcos's leg. It appeared to be filled with bedclothes. Jake nodded at it and said:

"What's in the bolsa, Marcos?"

Marcos seemed to stiffen, his eyes moving evasively, and Jake felt pleased for having hit a nerve. Marcos shrugged.

"Things I need to take home. I have to return to my family for a few days." Marcos took a pull at his beer bottle then waved it at the bartender.

"It looks like a sheet. Or pillows."

Marcos frowned at the plastic sack as though he wasn't quite sure what it contained. Finally he shrugged and said:

"It's a shroud for my father. Let me buy you a beer, Jake."

The bus was late, and Marcos kept buying beers for them both and shots of tequila for himself, which Jake refused. But Jake stayed to keep Marcos company. His father had died, and it was obvious he didn't want to be alone. This was charity work, Jake told himself, to be rewarded later. He even asked the usual questions, to give Marcos a chance to talk about his father:

"Was he an old man?"

"Had he been ill?"

"Were you close to him?"

But Marcos did not want to talk about him. He would answer in Spanish, "Más o menos," and direct the conversation back to women. But the beer and tequila were making him philosophical.

"They come, and they go. The bus comes, the bus goes. The women in one's life are exchanged—mother for sweetheart, sweetheart for wife, wife for lover. But compadres are forever."

Marcos put another cigarette in his mouth, lifted the matches from the bar, and dropped them to the floor. As he bent to pick them up, he started tipping forward, and Jake had to right him.

"Easy."

"Gracias, amigo."

Marcos managed to get the cigarette lit after spoiling four matches. He spoke now in Spanish:

"Hombre a hombre. Así es la vida. Así es la realidad. Compadres, hermanos, amigos. Fathers, sons, holy ghost."

"Marcos! Ven!"

It was the bartender calling. A battered blue bus had pulled into the plaza. Marcos stepped from the rail, staggered, and laid a hand on Jake's shoulder.

"Help me, compadre."

Jake nodded, and Marcos put his arm around his waist. The two men made their way to the door and out into the sun, arm in arm, like two compadres on a borrachera, and Jake felt Marcos's fingertips dig into his ribs.

Marcos leaned against the side of the bus while Jake bought his ticket from the driver. Jake then walked him up the steps and down the aisle to an empty seat in back as the driver climbed in and started the engine. Jake endured a parting embrace, made his way back down the aisle, and leapt from the bus as it pulled away in a ball of dust and black smoke. He saw Marcos through the window, saw him holding his face in his hands.

"Espera! Espera! Wait!"

Jake turned as the bartender came running out of the cantina with the green plastic bolsa that had been sitting at Marcos's side. The bartender saw the bus moving from the plaza, shrugged, and held the sack out to Jake.

Jake raised his hands, as if the man had pointed a gun at him.

The day got off to a foul start for the chief of police and kept going downhill from there.

First, brushing his teeth in the bathroom he hit a nerve that seemed to run down his spine to his cojones and made him howl as though he'd been kicked there.

Then, without explanation, his wife did not show up at breakfast, and their servant, Josefina, almost threw his plate of chilaquiles at him. When he called to her for more coffee, she came from the kitchen to pour it, scowled at him, and returned to her chores without speaking. He chewed on the right side of his mouth, but the hot coffee hit the exposed nerve.

Next, as the chief came through the door of the presidencia, Sergeant Rosales handed him a note saying that Revolutionary Party leader Don Pablo Martínez wished to see him today. Muñoz cursed and moved down the hall toward his office, where he saw Jesús Balderas Banyón, the waiter at the Café Cristóbal Colón, pacing outside his door.

"Tengo que hablar contigo inmediatamente, Jefe. I must ask a great favor."

Jesús followed the chief into his office and closed the frosted glass door behind him.

"As a friend," he whispered, "I beg you to arrest me."

Muñoz frowned. "Do you have problems with the narcotraficantes?"

Jesús shook his head. "No, worse. With my wife, Marielos, should she find out."

Muñoz nodded at the chair across from his desk and hung his gun belt on the hat tree in the corner. Jesús sat on the edge of the chair.

"You know the gringa with the Cessna, who lives on the hill?"

Muñoz sat on the front of his desk top, nodding. "Sí, sí. The flying whore of Texas."

"Exactamente. Two days ago she came into the cafe for comida and drank two brandies with coffee after dinner, and we talked. Then I went to her house, and she dressed me up as a cowboy, with boots, spurs, and a tall hat. She left the room and came back naked—except for a saddle and bridle—and handed me a whip. I said to myself, 'Why not, if this is what she wants?' . . ."

Muñoz took a cigarette from his tunic pocket and offered one to Jesús.

"Gracias. We drank more brandy, and the fiesta continued, and when we were finished . . . Pues, mira."

Cigarette in mouth, Jesús stood, turned, and pulled up his shirt to reveal a checkerboard of red welts on his slim, brown back. He loosened his belt and dropped his pants a few inches to show the chief his scarred buttocks.

Muñoz shook his head. Being police chief in a Mexican town was purgatory. Being chief in a Mexican town with a colony of idle gringos was hell.

"Tell me, Jesús. Why should I arrest you for this?"

"Because I have not made love to Marielos for two days, and she is getting suspicious."

Two days! Muñoz thought to himself. It had probably been two months since his wife was in the mood. Then in his mind he pictured Jesús's young wife, Marielos. She was right for wondering how any man with the opportunity could keep his hands off her for more than two minutes. Jesús continued:

"But if I spend a night in the bote, then I can say the marks came from guards who confused me with a child molester."

Muñoz looked away from Jesús, his eyes falling on the photograph of General Francisco Villa, who seemed to look down on him disapprovingly from the wall where he hung above an old army cot. Muñoz pressed out his cigarette in the ashtray on his desk.

"Mira, joven. How old are you?"

"Twenty-six."

"And how long have I been chief of police?"

"Siempre."

"And in all those years have you once known of any prisoner who was beaten or tortured in my jail?"

Jesús shrugged. "But it is normal."

"Not in my jail. Here we do not provide such services. If you wish to convince your wife that your whip marks came from the hands of vicious captors and not from playing horsey with the flying whore, I suggest you go to the commandant of the drug soldiers. He will be most happy to oblige."

Jesús sat up straight, the blood draining from his face.

There was a knock at the frosted door, and Muñoz saw the silhouette of Sergeant Rosales.

"Pásale."

The door opened and Rosales stood at attention and saluted.

"Sí, sargento."

"I have just received a telephone dispatch. There has been a shooting . . ." Rosales paused and lifted his chin. "Arriba!"

"Más despacio, por favor," said Muñoz to Sergeant Rosales. "The dead can wait."

Rosales let the police car slow on the steep incline and downshifted as Muñoz admired the brilliant red-pink bougainvillea growing over a white wall on the right. Behind the wall he glimpsed a three-story white house with red-tiled roof and, next to it, behind another white wall, a peach-colored hacienda with tall palms and a satellite dish.

It was bad enough that the gringos wore short pants, ruined the Mexican girls, and drove up the price of liquor. But they also bought up the land on the hill with the best views of the valley and the sunsets, then sat inside watching television. It was beyond comprehension.

Rosales pulled the undersized sedan to a stop at number 12, marked by a high, lime-colored wall and dark green metal gates standing ajar. Muñoz pried himself from the front seat, and Rosales came around the car to join him. The chief said:

"Wait here."

As much as Muñoz might have loved thinning out the gringo population in a gun battle, he loved himself more and had too many unknown pleasures to live for to allow his ambitious sergeant to follow him in with a loaded revolver.

Muñoz edged through the green doors into a cobbled court-yard with tall pines. In the driveway sat a black, late-model Mercedes station wagon with California plates. He circled it and saw a white-bearded man sitting on the front stoop with a gun in his right hand and a book in his left. The nickel-plated automatic hung loosely in his palm, and a bottle of good gin sat between his knees on the front steps. Muñoz stood by the car and called:

"Señor . . . Señor Whiteman?"

The man looked up, and Muñoz saw that his eyes were red, as though he had been crying. When the man saw the chief, he raised his gun and waved him over with it.

Muñoz swallowed and called out in English:

"Please put your gun down on the stair by the bottle . . . Now pick up the bottle. Gracias."

Muñoz approached with hands held at his sides and reached down between the legs of Mr. Whiteman to grab the pistol. He released the clip from the handle and checked the chamber. Both empty. Just fired. And it was not yet nine a.m.

The gringo took a drink from the bottle and looked up at Muñoz.

"I don't know why I did it. I just did it." He hung his head. "Drunk. Stupid drunk."

"Where is it?"

Whiteman wiped his eyes on his sleeve and pointed with the bottle toward the car. Muñoz walked back to the station wagon and gazed through the windows. Then he turned to Whiteman and raised his palms.

"Where is the body?"

Whiteman leaned back. "Body? What body?"

"The body of the person you shot."

Whiteman shook his head. "No person. Car. I shot the fucking car."

Muñoz turned back and noticed now the bullet holes in the black hood and fenders. California. America. Gringos.

Although Muñoz had been born there, held a U.S. as well as a Mexican passport, and spent three years in the U.S. Army, he never came to understand gringos and their rigid Anglo-Saxon mentality. They tried to harness the wind. Which led to blowups like this one.

"Rosales!"

His sergeant peeked through the green gates, and Muñoz motioned him over.

"Ven. Dime: Recibiste la llamada?"

"Sí, Jefe, I took the call."

"En español?"

"Más o menos."

"Okay."

Muñoz patted him on the shoulder and sent him back outside. Then he went over and sat down on the steps next to the gringo.

"Maybe I should keep your gun awhile. You can come to the presidencia for it when you feel it is safe."

"I try. I really try. I'm just a goddamn alcoholic." Whiteman held out the book to Muñoz: *How to Get Sober and Stay That Way.* "You'd think I could learn."

"That looks like a good book for you, Señor Whiteman. You should read it."

"Read it?" Whiteman slapped the book twice with the palm of his hand. "I wrote it."

Muñoz took it from him. On the back was a photo of Whiteman in which he appeared twenty years younger. The chief raised his eyebrows and nodded at the book in appreciation as Whiteman took another pull from the gin bottle. He then held the bottle out to Muñoz, who hesitated, then grabbed it and took a swig.

He wiped his lips on his shirt sleeve and explained to the drunk: "Already it has not been a good day."

Hector Muñoz Pineda stepped through the open doorway of the Café Cristóbal Colón and lifted his chin at Don Pablo Martínez, sitting as usual at his corner table.

In theory Muñoz reported to the mayor, but in fact it was Martínez who ran things in the pueblito. He controlled the municipality's ruling Revolutionary Party, an organization devoted, seemingly, to Martínez's control of the Revolutionary Party. Martínez handpicked the town's elected officials, including police chief. And although he always picked Muñoz, the chief still thought Don Pablo an asshole, perhaps because Muñoz's wife was forever reminding him of his obligation to the son of a bitch.

Don Pablo indicated the chair across from him. Muñoz threw his cap on the table and sat.

"Qué dia! Ya está bien chingado."

"Problemas?"

"Gringos!"

Don Pablo smiled. "But the gringos are very important to the economy of the pueblito."

"Fuck them and their greenbacks. I wish to send them all back to Toronto and New Jersey in pine boxes."

"With time we shall, Hector."

Jesús came over with coffee but refused to look at the chief.

Martínez asked: "How goes your investigation?"

Muñoz winced as the hot coffee hit the bad tooth, which he had momentarily forgotten. So that was why Don Pablo wanted to see him: Pancho's murder.

"All investigations are progressing well. I have hopes for quick resolution of all pending cases."

"Y la investigación del homicidio? When will you make an arrest?"

Don Pablo was understandably eager for him to arrest someone, Muñoz knew, in order to stop the rumors about his niece, who many thought had bashed in her fiancé's skull. But Muñoz had little physical evidence. All of Pancho's sculptures had been thrown to the floor and destroyed, yet no fingerprints other than the sculptor's had been found on the items. A seeming act of passion, but none of his suspects had directly passionate motives.

The niece could have escaped the arranged marriage easily enough if that had been her desire. The gringo she now slept with apparently had not even known her before the murder, but he was acquainted with the Negro artist, Freeman. Though possibly insane, Freeman possessed a motivation—to retain a run-down hacienda where he had painted an amateurish mural—that hardly seemed murderous. Likewise for the taxista, Guillermo Peralta. If Guillermo had been like most dying men, he would have been the last to admit it, the last to recognize that he had nothing to lose. Thus Muñoz had no good suspects. He said to Don Pablo:

"I expect an arrest any day now. Perhaps even tomorrow—or sooner."

Don Pablo nodded. "Bueno. Last night I had a dream. In it the whole town openly ridiculed me and the administration of the municipality. Even the campesinos insulted me in the street, accusing me of incompetence and corruption. There was no water, no electricity, and gun battles in the streets. And every time I tried to correct a problem, it only got worse—everything I touched turned to mierda. It was not a dream, Muñoz, but a nightmare."

It was not a nightmare, thought Muñoz, but reality, and he reached reflexively for his jaw as another pang ran from the bad tooth to his balls.

"Chihuahua!"

"Tooth?"

Muñoz nodded.

"Go see Doctor Rodríguez, Hector. Tell him I sent you."

Muñoz parked the police car on the street in front of the dentist's house and moved up the walk to the reception. In the waiting room three women sat silently with their children on metal folding chairs. A teenage girl in a white nurse's dress rose from behind a desk and bowed to the chief of police. Muñoz asked:

"Está aquí el doctor?"

A whirring noise came from behind the closed door to the girl's right, and her eyes moved there momentarily. She nodded.

"Please ask if I may see him for a little moment."

The girl went through the closed door and soon returned with Rodríguez following. The dentist pulled off a white rubber glove, and the two men shook hands.

"How good to see you, Hector."

"Buenos dias, Rafael."

Muñoz showed him the tooth, bending his knees while Rodríguez stood on tiptoe. The dentist shook his head.

"Está muy mal."

"When can you pull it?"

"Right now."

Muñoz lifted his head toward the women. "When will you finish with these?"

Rodríguez glanced at the line of patients in the metal chairs then at his watch.

"A la una. Come at one o'clock; then you can stay for comida."

Muñoz doubted that he would feel much like eating afterward, but nodded anyway and replaced his cap.

"Gracias. Very kind."

Outside, a woman in a black dress stood beside his police car. Muñoz tipped his hat.

"Buenos dias."

The woman nodded and said:

"I do not wish to bother you with my petty troubles, Chief Muñoz, but I have gotten no satisfaction from Doctor Rodríguez or his wife. Please look at this."

She led him across the narrow, cobbled street to a twenty-year-old Chevrolet and gestured at a dent in the back fender. The heavy steel bumper was also bent.

"They refuse to pay and even deny that they are responsible."

Muñoz squatted down and made a show of carefully examining the damage.

"When did this occur?"

"Months ago. The doctor says he was out of town at a conference when it happened, and his wife says I am lying. But I saw it. I was not yet asleep, and I heard the noise and looked out the window. And there was the car against mine."

"The doctor's car?"

There was a silence. Then she said:

"The doctor owns no car. But it had backed from his driveway. Therefore he is responsible for damages."

"Did you see it come from his driveway?"

"As I said, I did not rise until I heard the noise. But where else could it come from? Cars do not travel down the street sideways."

"Of course not. Obviously it must have come from the doctor's driveway. What make of automobile was it?"

"To me they all look the same."

"A new car or an old car?"

She shrugged.

"What color was it then?"

Again a pause. Then: "It was dark."

"The car was dark?"

"The night was dark. All I could see were the lights of the car."

"Then did you see the driver?"

She shook her head.

Muñoz stood and brushed his hands together.

"I am sorry, señora, but without some way of identifying the car or its driver, there is little I can do."

She took an envelope from her dress pocket and held it out to him. Muñoz raised his hands.

"And what is this?"

"The license plate number of the criminal's car."

Muñoz took the envelope, thanked her, and drove off thinking that if not for gringos and Mexicans and rotten teeth, his life could be quite pleasant.

"No, nada más," scratched the dispatcher's voice. "Only that it was 'a public offense to morals and decency.' She hung up before I could ask her name."

"Bueno," said Muñoz into the handset. "I'll go see."

He tossed the instrument on the dashboard and made a left turn. "Public" was the key word. His pueblito was a swamp of immorality and indecency. But as long as it was kept behind closed doors, he was content. He tried to do as much with his own immorality and indecency. But it was a small town, and what one intended to be private often became public.

Muñoz pulled the blue-and-white police car to the curb at a sign that read "Galeria de Arte Popular," slid from behind the wheel, and replaced his cap on his head. The front door and windows of the shop were open, and inside he could see the owner, Efrin Hernández, and the Negro artist, Jordan Trice Freeman, at work hanging a painting. The chief stepped up to the curb and stood in the doorway shaking his head.

After a moment Efrin turned and saw him.

"Jefe! Qué sorpresa!"

Efrin came to him in a cloud of scent, bracelets dangling from both arms, and extended a hand. The chief took it.

"Hola, joven. Como estás?"

"Bien. Muy bien. Business is so much better. Muchísimo mejor. And now we have an opening tomorrow night . . ." Efrin swept his hand around the room to indicate the newly hung canvases.

Muñoz again shook his head. "Jóvenes, jóvenes . . ."

Jordan came over. "Is there a problem?"

Muñoz shrugged. "Yes and no. No, there is not a problem when a man shakes his prick behind the door of his own home. Yes, there is a problem when he does it on the street." Muñoz lifted his chin at the series of paintings depicting black penises. "This is shaking your prick in public."

Jordan stood tense, fists clenched. Muñoz glared at him and thought: Please take a swing at me and thus improve my day of shit, so that I might break thy thumbs. Por favor.

But Freeman stood fast and said in English:

"I've gotta have this show. I need to sell some paintings. I need some fucking money."

Muñoz shrugged and stepped toward him. "That's your fucking problem, amigo."

Efrin moved between the two men and clapped his hands together.

"I have an idea: a private showing. By invitation only."

Muñoz spread his hands and turned briefly toward people passing on the street.

"Sure. As long as your customers can get in without opening the door."

Efrin hesitated, then said:

"In the workshop. We'll hang them in the back room."

Muñoz stared at Efrin a moment then said:

"That's all I ask: behind closed doors."

The chief took a last look at the line of penises in various stages of erection. He turned away and moved toward the sidewalk. But when he got to the doorway he paused and turned back to the artist.

"I have a question. Why do you suddenly need money? You have lived in my town for years without ever selling a painting."

Muñoz could see the black man's ears turning red.

"I need to get to New York."

"So suddenly?"

"My brother died."

"Then your leaving has nothing to do with the murder of the sculptor Pancho?"

Once, on his way to a convention in Oaxaca, Muñoz noticed a sign posted inside the bus over the driver's head: "Do not leave your trash on the bus. Throw it out the window." Ever since, he had tried to live by those words. If his day was shit, the best he could do was spread it around.

The Negro seemed to blanch but said nothing.

Muñoz said, "Maybe Nueva York is the place for you, hombre," and he moved out the door to squeeze once more inside his car.

Sergeant Rosales put the day's mail in the center of the chief's desk as Muñoz tossed his cap on the hat tree in the corner of the office.

"Here, Rosales." Muñoz handed him the envelope from Doctor Rodríguez's neighbor. "Find out who owns this car."

The letter on top of the stack on his desk bore the seal of the army of the United States of Mexico, and Muñoz muttered to himself, "Chinga tu . . ."

Standing by his desk, he slit it open with a switchblade knife he carried in his pants pocket, unfolded the one-page letter inside, and saw the signature of the commandant of the army drug enforcement unit stationed in the old monastery outside town. The general no longer spoke to Muñoz; their only communication was terse, official documents such as this one demanding a prisoner the municipal police had arrested on cocaine possession charges.

Muñoz placed the letter in a wire basket on his desk and looked up to see Sergeant Rosales standing by the door.

"Jefe, hay un gringo, un Señor Harting, a verle."

"Sobre qué?"

"About a prisoner."

"The American drug user?"

"No, a drunken servant."

Muñoz tossed the switchblade on his desk. "Why not? One crazy gringo more or less cannot much alter the downward course of my day. Send him to me."

After a moment Jake Harting came through the door, and Muñoz gestured toward the chair across from him. Jake sat, and

Muñoz lowered himself into his wooden desk chair.

"Muchas gracias, Señor Muñoz, por su tiempo."

"De nada. You can speak English if you wish, Mr. Harting."

Jake nodded stone-faced.

"I've come to see you about Bonifacio Aviles, the gardener at the house where I rent a room. He was arrested last week for public drunkenness. I tried to pay the fine, but the sergeant told me he can't be released until you say he is ready."

"That is correct."

"But he's certainly sober by now."

Muñoz nodded. "Yes, however he is no longer under arrest for public drunkenness. He is under arrest for making death threats."

"Bonifacio? Against whom?"

"Against his wife and his best friend, who are now living together."

Jake shook his head. "But his wife left him months ago."

"Sí, but last week, while Bonifacio was away, she came and took his trumpet and sold it to buy new clothes for her boyfriend. Now, without the trumpet, Bonifacio cannot play in the mariachi band. He says he would rather kill them both and die for it than see his family starve. I think it is the music, not the earnings, that he cannot live without. However, until he withdraws his threat I cannot very well let him out on the street to kill them."

"Do you really think he would?"

"I think he might try, and possibly get himself killed or wound innocent bystanders. But as long as he is in my custody, he will stay out of trouble."

Jake looked at Muñoz for a moment and said:

"Then the only problem is the trumpet."

"Sí. I think he is secretly glad to be rid of the woman."

"Good. Then I'll find a new one today and bring it."

That's what Muñoz liked about America: money was no problem. It solved problems. You spent it and got some more. He pursed his lips.

"Tal vez, tal vez. I will talk to Bonifacio. If he agrees to behave—and I see that he is sincere—he is free to go as soon as he has the trumpet."

Jake stood. "Gracias."

Muñoz lifted a finger in the air.

"One other thing, Harting. I understand you are friends with Marta Martínez, the former fianceé of the dead sculptor Pancho . . ."

Jake nodded.

". . . and with the Negro artist, Jordan Freeman."

He shrugged.

"Tell me, Harting, who do you think killed Pancho?"

Muñoz saw the gringo bite his lip. He shrugged and shook his head, but he had an idea. He wasn't saying, but Muñoz saw he had an idea.

Only four prisoners remained that morning in the hold-over cell, a large square cage with a stone floor. The others—the usual array of campesinos and cowboys who came to market, drank grain alcohol or pulque, and passed out in the street—had slept it off and been released at dawn.

Two of the prisoners slept curled together on the floor in the center of the cage. The drug offender squatted against the bars to the right of the sliding door. Muñoz walked up behind him and tapped the bars with his keys. The young blond-haired man looked up over his shoulder at Muñoz but did not stir.

"Stand up," Muñoz said in English.

The man stood and turned, and Muñoz could smell the stale perspiration in his clothes. Once they might have been good clothes, but now they were streaked with grime and ripped at the elbows and knees, as if he might have resisted arrest. Like his clothes, the young man might have had some utility in him at one time, though Muñoz doubted it. Muñoz believed in fate and character and luck, and this hombre just had strike three.

"I have just received orders to release you . . ."

"About time!"

". . . to the military antidrug force"—he lifted his chin over his shoulder—"billeted outside town."

The young man leaned back and stared at Muñoz as though trying to gauge his sincerity. Muñoz remained silent.

"The army? What for?"

"Interrogation."

"About what? I don't know anything—except that your men planted some stuff on me. I can tell them that."

"I very strongly suggest that you tell them the truth—who you got it from and how much you paid—and tell them quickly."

"I won't say anything until I have legal counsel."

Muñoz shook his head. He had had this conversation before. It always went this way. It always went badly.

"Where are you from, joven?"

"The States. Michigan."

"Then you must recognize that this is not Michigan. This is Mexico. Here you have no rights. Here you have nothing to protect you but God, and I suggest you start praying to him."

The young man's lower lip trembled, but soon he straightened it. "You're threatening me. Trying to scare me. You're in with them."

Muñoz stood with hands on hips, looking through the bars at the young man. Pobrecito. You poor, stupid bastard. The chief shook his head.

"No, joven, I'm with you. Believe it or not, I am on your side. But I am the only one on your side, so I suggest you listen to me, for I mean to tell you how to stay alive over the next twenty-four hours."

The man from Michigan pressed his knees together, and Muñoz turned away. It was a lousy world and a lousy day for all involved, and he could not stand there and look at the Michigano's face as he pissed his pants. Muñoz spied Bonifacio Aviles leaning against the far side of the cage and moved there.

The gardener took off his hat as Muñoz approached.

"Buenos dias, Jefe."

"Buenos."

Aviles held his hat in front of him, licked his lips, and looked at the chief. He was a short, thin man, and Muñoz wondered how such a meek creature survived in such a hard country. By swallowing wagonloads of mierda, that was the answer, Muñoz knew. By kissing culos right and left. By stepping off the sidewalk into the gutter when a caballero passed; by never questioning orders given a servant. And now this.

"Mira, Bonifacio. The gringo who lives at the house of Señora Pola López . . ."

The gardener nodded and held his hand a foot over his head. "Sí, sí. El grande. Señor Jaque."

"Yes. He came to see me and has offered to replace your stolen trumpet."

The man grabbed the bars in front of him. "De veras?"

"Sí. And when he does, then perhaps I can release you."

"Qué milagro!"

"Pero hay tres condiciones." Muñoz held up three fingers.

"First, you must withdraw the threat against your wife and her lover; second, you must never go to their house or molest them in any way; third, you must change the lock on your door so she cannot steal your new trumpet as well."

"A new trumpet?"

"Yes, brand new."

Bonifacio raised his hand as though taking an oath. "I swear on the Virgin of Guadalupe: I will do as you ask." He crossed himself.

"Bueno. But I must keep you here until the gringo shows up with the instrument."

Bonifacio smiled. "No hay problema. Estoy contento."

Muñoz tried to return the smile but did not do so well. He moved back to the other side of the cage to continue his conversation with the young man from Michigan.

Muñoz touched his tongue to the place where his tooth used to be and lifted his glass toward his friend Rafael Rodríguez.

"Me parece bien. It feels much better, doctor."

"The tequila will help as well. Salud!"

Señora Rodríguez stepped down into the sala from the dining room in a becoming blue dress.

"Good afternoon, Chief Muñoz."

"Buenas tardes, señora."

She moved to her husband and took his hand. He said to her:

"Something to drink, Ilena?"

"No, gracias, dinner is nearly ready."

They followed her back up the three steps into the dining room, and Muñoz thought, what a lovely ass. She was somewhat younger than her husband, perhaps thirty-five, and Muñoz wondered if she dressed that way for comida every day or if she had done so only on his account. She wore dark nylons, red high-heel shoes, gold earrings, and a warm smile. No wonder Rafael always seemed so cheerful. Muñoz recalled his own wife's absence at the breakfast table that morning and wondered what it signaled.

An Indian woman with braided hair served the meal, and Rodríguez poured red wine. The room was cool and the table covered by a white linen cloth. Rodríguez raised his glass:

"To marriage and happiness."

He and Ilena touched fingertips on the tablecloth and looked into each other's eyes. Muñoz raised his glass: To marriage or happiness, he silently amended the toast. He might better tolerate the fact that his wife was not so young as Ilena and did not have her perfect ass if only she would smile like Ilena once a day. I do not ask much, Lord.

They ate roast goat and rice with peas. The wine felt like velvet on his tongue. Muñoz smiled at Señora Rodríguez, and she smiled back.

"Tell us, Chief Muñoz, how go things in our pueblito? Are we safe from vandals and thieves these days?"

"Please, señora: Hector. Call me Hector."

He had known Rodríguez for fifteen years, ever since the dentist first returned to town with his bride to begin his practice. Muñoz had met Señora Rodríguez many times since and had often admired her from afar during Mass. Yet this was the first time he had been invited for dinner. She replied:

"But only if I may be Ilena to you."

Muñoz nodded and winked as he chewed.

"Do not fear, Ilena. You and yours are safe. Just lock your gates at night and stay away from gringos."

"Claro!"

Doctor Rodríguez leaned forward. "And how goes the investigation?"

Damn. He could have enjoyed his dinner quite well without being reminded of "the investigation." It recalled to Muñoz his conversation that morning with Don Pablo, in which he promised an arrest. "Perhaps even tomorrow—or sooner," he had said. Híjole! If not for his big mouth and his hard tamale, life could be so simple. Rodríguez smiled at him and waited. So did Ilena, and Muñoz smiled back.

"The investigation goes very well. I expect an arrest at any time—perhaps even today, even as we dine!"

Good. Well done, Muñoz. Now Rafael will tell his patients, the whole town will await an arrest, and you will appear a bigger fool than ever when nothing happens. But at least you are consistent.

The doctor and his wife again touched hands and smiled at each other. Such happiness. Muñoz sat chewing gingerly on the right side of his mouth, picturing the perpetual scowl on his wife's face. In his mind he tried to change it to a smile, but it would not budge.

Chief Muñoz decided to leave his car in the street in front of the dentist's house and walk the few blocks down the hill for a drink at the Legión Americana. It felt good to stretch his legs after the meal and enjoy the quietest time of day.

He passed shops shuttered for the afternoon and, through barred windows, heard dinner dishes being cleared away. Inside the thick stone walls people were lowering themselves into hammocks or onto cool sheets in darkened rooms. And some were making love, Muñoz was reminded as he passed a little boy who had been caged on a sill between window bars and closed shutters. The child cried aloud, announcing to neighbors that his parents were in bed together behind the shutters, and Muñoz said to him as he passed:

"Tranquilo, vaquero. Silencio. You will have your turn some-day."

As Muñoz turned left at the mercado, an old campesino leading a burro with sacks of soil tied to its back stopped and saluted the chief. Muñoz returned the salute.

"Buenas tardes, grandfather."

He heard the clack of billiard balls as he strolled past the open doorway of El Club Deportivo. In the middle of the next block, he pushed through a wooden door into a shaded court-yard and tossed his cap into the center of one of four metal card tables set along the left wall.

Through a doorway to the right, in the saloon of the Ameri-can Legion, he saw the self-help author Jonathan C. Whiteman with his head on the bar. Another white-haired gringo on the barstool next to him seemed to be having an argument with Señor Whiteman, albeit one-sided. My comrades in arms, thought the chief.

A turning point, his being drafted into the U.S. Army after escaping Mexican conscription. When he had learned enough English, he moved from sniper to M.P., which led to the civil-ian police and ultimately to his current post. For better or worse. There were days when he wished he had become an outlaw instead. Today.

Muñoz pulled a metal folding chair out from the table and sat in the shade along the wall. A yellow warbler flitted about a nest in an avocado tree growing from the center of the brick-floor patio, and an iridescent green hummingbird fed at the bright red bougainvillea climbing over the wall. The bartender saw him through the open door and waved, and soon a young

woman in a white blouse and black skirt appeared in the doorway. When she saw who it was she called:

"Cerveza, Jefe?"

Muñoz nodded, and soon she reappeared carrying a metal
tray with brown bottle and glass, moving toward Muñoz, her
hips swaying in the black skirt, smiling, and he smiled back.

She was twenty-five, she said, and almost slender and very
Indian. And though she did not have the polish or the Spanish
ass of the dentist's wife, she was a good and desirable woman.
There. That was one good thing in his day, Muñoz told himself. At least there was Altagracia, and he looked about for some
wood to knock on so as not to jinx that, too, but all he found
within reach was either metal or stone.

She stood over him pouring the beer, and Muñoz looked
up and asked: "Algo de tomar?"

She smiled even wider and laid a hand on his shoulder.

"No, gracias, Hector. I am no longer drinking alcohol."

The tequila and wine from dinner made him yawn. Muñoz
stared at her and felt something odd. It was the feeling he got
when he knew a suspect wanted to confess. He lit a cigarette
and said:

"Does this mean we will no longer get drunk and play
together?"

Altagracia sat in the chair to his left and reached across to
touch the hand that held the cigarette.

"I am going to have a child."

Muñoz raised the cigarette to his lips.

"En serio?"

"Truly. I went yesterday to the mothers' clinic and they
made tests. Qué milagro!"

Muñoz smiled back. Yes, it was a miracle. He had five daughters—all nearly grown—with the scowling one on the other

side of town. He had yet another wife in exile in Laredo along with a young son and daughter. Now this. Muñoz thought it very Mexican.

"Es mio?"

"Claro! Of course it's yours. Who else?"

Muñoz shrugged. "The mothers' clinic, you said?"

She nodded.

"If you would have told me, I could have taken you to be examined at the hospital in San Juan."

Altagracia dropped her eyes and stared at her hands in her lap, and Muñoz wished he hadn't said it. It was unnecessary and stupid of him to mention it. She had already gone to the mothers' clinic, and that could not be changed. But as a result, now the whole town would know, and he saw that was what she wanted, to walk pregnant down the street with everyone whispering that she carried the child of Chief of Police Hector Muñoz Pineda. He reached across and took her hand.

"No llora, bonita. Don't cry. I will see you get the best of care, and we will have a fine child. Everything will be fine."

Just fine. But how? He was thinking about it when something made him look up.

José, the bartender, stood in the doorway of the saloon waving to get the chief's attention. Then he made a gesture of holding an invisible telephone receiver to his ear.

Muñoz moved the police sedan over a dirt road between dusty nopales, then past a village of five mud-brick homes with pigs rooting in the yard. He shook his head at the barren countryside, wondering how the people managed to survive. Then, of course, some didn't.

The call at the bar had come from Sergeant Rosales, after which Muñoz had walked slowly back up the hill to his car parked at the house of Doctor Rodríguez. Then he had driven out on the main highway and turned onto a cobbled road, where he passed towns named Rincón de Purgatorio, Malaguas, and Infierno—Corner of Purgatory, Badwater, and Hell—noting how less poetic things sounded when he translated them into English. He had stopped at a nameless village where no one knew anything about a dead body in an arroyo and had to call in to Rosales to straighten out his directions.

Now he saw the blue-and-white Volkswagen of the municipal police resting with its doors open at the bottom of the gully ahead of him. Muñoz stopped the sedan at the top of the hill to walk down.

Patrolman Eduardo García slid from the Volkswagen, bent to pick up a stone, and hurled it at a pack of dogs creeping down the other side of the gully. When García turned back and saw Muñoz coming down the hill, he reached inside the car for his uniform cap. Children came running from the village after Muñoz, who promptly told them to go inside. García saluted the chief, who laid a hand on his shoulder.

"Donde está, joven?"

He followed García through a seeming garbage dump: tin cans, broken bottles, and plastic sacks. White bones.

"The dogs had dug it up and were feeding. The children found it, and one of the men came to town on his bicycle. It is a young man. Nude. Not so pretty now."

Muñoz stood above the corpse, hands on hips.

"Not much of a grave," he said. "They must have been in a hurry."

"Claro."

The corpse was swollen and blue, and García was right: not so pretty. Muñoz squatted and held the dead man's hand, and it was stiff and cold. The doctor would tell him when he last breathed.

"Mira, García. Here, on the wrists, and on the ankles, too. Marks. Ropes or handcuffs. And the throat."

"Strangled?"

"No sé. Let's turn him over."

They rolled the corpse over so it lay face down. On the buttocks were seeming whip marks, caked brown blood, and feces. Much blood.

García looked at Muñoz. "Qué pasó?"

"La sodomía."

"Mande?"

Muñoz explained it to García, and the patrolman's eyes widened.

"Homos?"

"Maybe. Perhaps he was playing games with others and an accident occurred. We will take his photo and show it to all the known homosexuals. But then there are the secret ones, the married ones, and the machos.

"Or maybe it was not that at all. Maybe he was killed because of drugs, and the other was just for fun. Or maybe it was a brother or a father or a husband taking revenge for a rape. Or perhaps the boy was an innocent, a worker returning from California with his earnings, set upon by thieves."

"Or maybe," said García, "he was questioned by the drug soldiers."

Muñoz looked at the young patrolman, a distant relative of Don Pablo Martínez, who two months earlier had requested a position for him. Muñoz had given García a nightstick and a uniform and the job of patrolling the outer reaches of the municipality, where there was never any trouble. The lad seemed content wearing the uniform and driving the old Beetle.

"Yes, there is that, too."

The dogs again approached, and Eduardo García pitched another stone at them. Muñoz felt himself gagging from the smell of the body.

"Good job, García. Guard the body well. The doctor and the photographer and the Cruz Roja should be here soon. When all is done, bring me a copy of your report personally."

García reached out toward the chief reflexively, as if to keep him from leaving, then checked himself.

"Pero . . ."

"What is it, García? Do you have report forms?"

"Sí, pero . . ."

Muñoz put his arm around the boy's shoulder to lead him back to the patrol car.

"Come. I will show you how to fill one out."

García stopped and looked to the chief with tears forming at the corners of his eyes.

"No puedo."

"You're not able? Why not?"

"I cannot write."

Muñoz looked at Don Pablo's relative and thought of Don Pablo beating on him that morning for an arrest.

"Can you read?"

"Un poco."

"Okay. I will give you a lesson while we wait for the doctor."

Stars were already showing themselves in the eastern sky as Muñoz's car reached the edge of town. The photographer had come, then the medical examiner, and finally the Red Cross ambulance to carry the body away. Muñoz had crossed himself as the doors on the van closed, then completed the official report with García's help.

But he sensed this would be one murder he would not solve. Most were easy. Crimes of passion, committed with ample witnesses to verify the assassin's vengeance. He would even solve the murder of the sculptor Pancho some day. But the killer of the mutilated boy in the campo would likely go free. If the youth had not lived nearby, then he would never be identified. He would be buried in an unmarked grave and soon forgotten, and there would be no justice. But life would go on.

The people of Muñoz's pueblito would go on with their daily routines feeling secure. They would see a facade of order and believe that all the laws of God and nature and the state were in full force and that they were protected. But Muñoz knew better.

His job was to help create that semblance of order: to patrol the streets with uniformed men and, when there was trouble, to dispatch cars with loud sirens and flashing lights and thus reassure the people. But he knew Mexico and knew that his work was a mere parade: a show of strength, pomp, and little more. There were two Mexicos: the Mexico of faith and innocence and sugar candies, of miracles and magic; and the Mexico of blood, matadors, and vengeance; of corruption and false honor; of savagery. It was the second Mexico that was his world, and he had lived in it too long to return to the first. There were no miracles, just self-delusion; no magic, just pretense.

The police car crept over the rutted road—perpetually under construction—that connected the main highway and his town. Muñoz moved the car slowly across the bridge spanning the fetid creek that ringed the barrio bajo, his headlights bouncing up the hill toward the center of town and down again as the car leveled, and a man in a cowboy hat and boots came dancing backward through the beams, stumbling and rolling head over heels until coming to a dead stop in the dust.

Muñoz stomped on the brakes and looked to his right through the open front door of the last pulque saloon in town.

"Goddamn pulquería!"

Only a few remaining rustics—cowboys and campesinos—actually preferred pulque, and this was the last bar in town that served it exclusively. Thanks to movies and television programs made in the capital, the tastes of the townsfolk had been elevated from the milky agave brew to cheap brandy with Coca-Cola and factory tequila with lime. Soon they would expect to make love to blonde women like the ones they saw on the television screen; soon they would require assault rifles instead of knives. Muñoz flipped on the flashing red roof-lights and reached beneath the seat for his nightstick.

Inside the tavern two cowboys had a third pinned against the bar, attempting to stand him up straight enough to throw punches at his face, which was already covered with blood. Three other vaqueros lay motionless on the floor—drunk, dead, or knocked unconscious, Muñoz did not know which. The owner stood behind the bar with a blasé look and a baseball bat. He gazed at Muñoz and shrugged.

"Ni modo."

It was one of the phrases that Muñoz could never translate well into English. "There's nothing to be done about it," or, "It doesn't matter," or something in between.

Muñoz saw that there was, in fact, little for the owner to be concerned about. There were neither tables nor chairs in his saloon, and he poured the pulque from five-gallon plastic gasoline cans into plastic cups. The windows had been boarded over.

Muñoz took a nickel-plated police whistle from his shirt pocket and blew.

"Oye!"

The boxers at the rail did not even turn around.

It had not been a good day. In fact, thought Muñoz, it had been a day washed in pure excrement. Yet now God had presented him with a gift: an opportunity to purge himself of all the wickedness and perversity that had infested him since dawn. Muñoz gritted his teeth, raised his nightstick over his head, and waded in.

Now it was all behind him. His hellish day was finally over.

He had put the cowboys in the can with the other drunks and the would-be musician Bonifacio Aviles, who waved to the chief and smiled, anticipating no doubt his impending release. But Muñoz doubted that the gringo would ever show with the promised trumpet. Gringos, he had found, were almost as bad as Mexicans at keeping their word.

As he was about to leave the room, Muñoz stopped, turned, and confirmed that the young man from Michigan had been transferred to the military for interrogation.

On his way out of the building, Muñoz was surprised to see Sergeant Rosales still behind his desk, concentrating on a book.

"Qué estudias?" Muñoz asked.

Rosales looked up and folded the book away.

"Nada."

"You were studying something."

"Más o menos."

"What?"

"English."

Ambition. A very dangerous thing, Muñoz thought. But all he said to Rosales was, "Go with God."

Muñoz started the engine of the patrol car and put it in gear. Rosales saw it: The chief was getting old. Too old to break up bar fights much longer. Too old to take orders from Pablo Martínez. Someday soon Muñoz might drink himself to death, and Rosales would be ready. Ready to deal with both Mexican and gringo. To keep the pretense of peace in this insane asylum of a town. Good. "He can have the damn job," Muñoz said aloud.

Muñoz pulled the police car into his driveway and locked the gates behind it, sealing the cordon that ringed his home, a twelve-foot-high brick wall topped with broken bottles embedded in concrete.

Inside the house he bolted the front door behind him before hanging his hat and his gun belt on the peg beside it. On the table by the door he saw that the latest edition of *Detecciones Fantásticas* had arrived in that day's mail. He put the magazine under his arm and went to the kitchen for a beer.

His wife was sitting up in bed wearing her reading glasses, writing a letter on the lap desk he had bought her last Christmas.

"Buenas noches, kitten."

She glanced at him momentarily but said nothing.

Muñoz put his beer and his magazine on the nightstand and kicked off his boots. He unbuckled his uniform trousers and had them nearly down to his knees when she said:

"What do you think you're doing?"

Muñoz straightened up with his pants around his knees. After a few seconds, he said:

"I am undressing to join my wife in bed."

She shook her head. "No you are not. If you wish to sleep with a woman, why not go to the sty of the whore from the American Legion?"

Muñoz closed his eyes and took a deep breath. He opened them and gazed at the comfortable bed and the cold beer and the *Detecciones Fantásticas* magazine. Then he nodded as with resignation, pulled up his pants, and found his boots. He took the beer and the magazine and went back out to the foyer to retrieve his gun and hat.

Muñoz parked the police car in front of the presidencia, grabbed his magazine from the seat, and walked up the block toward the Café Cristóbal Colón, whose lights fell to the dark street from an open doorway.

Jesús was turning the chairs upside-down on the tables as the busboy Homero mopped the red tile floor. When the waiter saw the chief in the doorway, he said:

"Lo siento, Jefe, the kitchen is closed. Pero . . ."

"Está bien. I wanted only a beer. Bring me six Negras."

Muñoz leaned against the jamb studying the cover of his magazine: A patrolman in Oaxaca foils a bank robbery. A bureaucrat in Guadalajara exposes road-construction kickbacks. In the State of Sinaloa, a police operation cracks a gang of narcotraficantes.

Muñoz let out a long sigh. And in a forgotten pueblito in the remotest reaches of the Bajío, a police chief teaches his patrolman to read and gets caught with his pants down.

Jesús returned with the beer, set it on the table, and handed Muñoz a dark blue book.

"Mira, Jefe. I have solved my problem."

Muñoz studied the spine of the book and frowned. "*El Libro del Mórmon?*"

"Sí. I am a convert. Thus the scars on my back, from the initiation ritual."

Muñoz shook his head. "I do not know the Mormons, but I do not believe flogging is part of their ceremony."

"Quién sabe? It is secret. Mira. See, a picture of the Lord preaching to the Aztecs."

"But Marielos is very Catholic."

"No problem. I will reconvert next week."

"You are serious."

"Very. She is a sweet girl, but I don't doubt that she could slit my throat, or worse, if she learned the truth."

Muñoz paid for the beer and headed back down the block to his office. The bells of the cathedral tower began to chime, and he looked up over the trees in the zócalo to the clock there. Ten. The longest of days.

The night sergeant and a sleepy patrolman stood and saluted as Muñoz entered the building.

"No radio-playing tonight, Cabrera."

"Sí, Jefe."

The door to his office was open. He flipped on the light, set the beer and the magazine on the cot against the wall, and went to the hat tree to hang up his gun belt.

On his desk were two messages: an invitation from the owner of the Galeria de Arte Popular, Efrin Hernández, to an exhibition of erotic art; and a note from Sergeant Rosales. The license plate number Muñoz had given him was assigned to a vehicle owned by a Francisco Aguilar. Muñoz shrugged and moved to the cot.

Muñoz lowered himself onto the cot and once again removed his boots. He opened a beer and, with *Detecciones Fantásticas* in his lap, leaned against the wall beneath the portrait of Villa.

The chief took a drink of dark beer from the bottle and flipped through the magazine, glancing at the lurid photographs of traffic fatalities and murder victims. Then he stopped and looked up. General Francisco Villa. Pancho Villa.

Francisco Aguilar. Pancho Aguilar.

Muñoz tossed the magazine aside, lurched forward, and sat erect with his bare feet on the cool stone floor. He sat perfectly still, like a Buddha, his eyes moving back and forth unfocused until, after nearly a minute, he muttered aloud:

"Madre de Dios!"

He pulled on his boots, cursing first the left then the right. Never had there been such a day in the history of law enforcement. Mierda completa. He would write it all down and send it to *Detecciones Fantásticas*. But they would never print it. It was too fantastic. They could never believe that one policeman could have such a bad day.

The metal gates topped with ornate wrought-iron designs were sealed tight and locked. Muñoz pressed a lighted bell switch beneath a metal speaker grille embedded in the stucco wall to the left, just below a hand-painted ceramic plate that read: "Casa Rodríguez."

Soon Muñoz heard a woman's singsong voice—the maid's—coming from the grille:

"Buenas noches. Para servirle."

"Está en la casa el señor?"

"Sí, pero . . . Quién es?"

"Hector Muñoz, policía municipal. Es urgente."

"Un momentito."

Muñoz waited. He studied the position of the dentist's driveway and turned to see where his neighbor parked her car. To do that kind of damage, one would have to be very careless, very distracted, or very drunk—or perhaps all three.

Muñoz waited, standing beside his police car, rubbing his chin nervously. It cannot get much worse, he told himself. But even as he said it, he knew it was a lie.

True, it had been a bad day for him—a miserable, aggravating, discouraging day. However, it was even worse for the drunken cowboys with blackened eyes and bruised skulls sleeping it off on the cold floor of the bote. For the gringo cocaine user now in the hands of the drug soldiers. And for Doctor Rafael Rodríguez. But Muñoz knew that for himself, at least, things had to get better.

A metal pedestrian door cut into the gate clicked open, and the Indian woman who had served him dinner stood aside.

"Pásele, señor."

"Gracias."

He waited while she closed the door behind him then followed her into the house.

There was no light in the sala, and she took him through the dim, unlit waiting room into the doctor's surgery. Muñoz squinted against the bright light and saw Rodríguez at the sink washing his hands. The dentist looked over his shoulder at Muñoz and nodded toward the large, hydraulic chair in the center of the room.

"Siéntese, Hector, and we'll have a look at it."

Muñoz stood holding his beige-and-black uniform cap in his hand; he hesitated, then lowered himself into the chair.

Rodríguez came to him pulling on latex gloves. He tilted back the chair, fixed a light on his patient, and stood over him with a probe in his hand. Muñoz opened his mouth.

Rodríguez frowned and touched the instrument to the area where he had pulled the tooth earlier that day.

"Hay dolor?"

"No."

The dentist touched another spot. "Aquí?"

Muñoz shook his head, and Rodríguez withdrew the probe from his mouth.

"Then where does it hurt you?"

Muñoz looked at him for a moment, then said:

"I did not come about the tooth, Rafael. I came about the dead sculptor, Pancho Aguilar."

The dentist stepped back, and Muñoz saw he had figured right. He had already known he was right. Now Rodríguez's face confirmed it. He had gone white, like a dead man.

"Pancho Aguilar? No lo conozco."

"No, you did not know him. But Ilena did. You did not meet him but once, I suppose. It was a very stupid thing you did, Rafael. Very stupid."

The dentist stomped his foot. "It was an accident, Hector. Believe me. I went to confront him with it, and we fought."

Muñoz shook his head and nodded toward the dentist's hands. "One does not wear rubber gloves only to have a discussion."

Rodríguez looked at his hands and appeared as if he was going to faint. Muñoz stood and helped him into the examination chair. Rodríguez took a deep breath, let it out, and turned to Muñoz.

"A husband has rights. He had seduced Ilena. A man must protect what is his."

Muñoz spread his hands. "I don't blame you for killing him, Rafael. I am sure he deserved it. But I do fault you for being so half-assed about it. Perhaps you could have planned to catch them at it and shoot him, make it look like a crime of passion . . ."

"It was a crime of passion!"

Rodríguez began to cry, and Muñoz put his hand on his

shoulder. "I know, Rafael. I know. But you made it look pre-meditated."

Rodríguez blurted out: "I wanted no one to know about Ilena and him, to wear the horns . . ."

"Yo entiendo. It is a bad business."

The dentist reached up and laid a hand on the chief's. "Must you arrest me, Hector? We have been friends for so long."

Muñoz looked at him and thought about dinner that after-noon with the doctor and his wife. The first time he had been invited in fifteen years, only to be questioned about the investi-gation. In his mind he saw the happy couple holding hands and smiling, drinking to marriage and happiness.

"I must."

"Perhaps if we went to Don Pablo first . . . He owes me a favor."

Muñoz shook his head. "Don Pablo has no say in police matters. I am sorry, Rafael, but I must take you with me."

"For how long?"

"Who knows? Perhaps Don Pablo knows a judge who owes him a favor. Perhaps others will allow that it was indeed a pas-sionate act. But that is not for me to decide."

"How long?"

"Perhaps just a few weeks or a few months. At worst just a few years."

"But Ilena . . ."

The dentist stopped there, but Muñoz saw his problem. He knew she would not remain faithful to him for several years. Perhaps not even for a few weeks. He would go mad in jail thinking about it. Muñoz nodded and said:

"Do not worry about Ilena. I will see that she is taken care of."

"Gracias. Gracias, amigo," said Rodríguez, and Muñoz saw what a sorry and trusting bastard the dentist truly was. Not a vicious criminal but a hapless cornudo. No, his was not a story for *Detecciones Fantásticas.*

Hector Muñoz Pineda did not now feel like sleeping. He stood in the doorway of the presidencia, feet spread, thumbs hooked in the belt that carried his handcuffs, handgun, and bullets. He looked out over the town square, above the manicured elms to the spire of the cathedral and its clock. Almost midnight.

He tried to think back over the previous twenty-four hours to something that might have jinxed him—a black cat, a ladder, a witch. Or maybe he was being punished for something wicked he had done. Muñoz thought about it for a minute but could not come up with anything substantive.

Just then he saw the silhouette of a man walking across the deserted zócalo carrying an oddly shaped suitcase. The man turned his head in Muñoz's direction as though he felt the chief's eyes on him and stopped dead. Then he came walking toward the open door of the presidencia where Muñoz stood.

The man came closer, moving under the dark elms and out into the glow of a streetlight, and Muñoz saw it was the gringo Jake Harting. He came across the street to Muñoz, stepped to the curb, and, without saying a word, knelt before the chief. He laid the rectangular case on the stone banqueta before him, slid aside the clasps, and opened the lid, revealing a gold-plated trumpet.

"Had to go all the way to Santa Ana for it. Then the damn bus broke down on the way back."

Muñoz bent forward, hands on knees.

"It is beautiful. Expensive?"

"Lo suficiente."

Muñoz put a hand on Jake's shoulder. "I owe you an apology and a drink, hombre. I did not think you would do it." Then he turned and called over his shoulder: "Cabrera! Traígame del bote a Bonifacio Aviles."

"El jardinero?"

"Sí."

After a minute Cabrera reappeared with the prisoner.

"Take off the esposas, Cabrera. Aviles is free."

The gardener spied the trumpet on the sidewalk and as soon as the handcuffs were off had the instrument in his hands.

"Qué linda! Gracias, Señor Jaque. Y a usted, Jefe. Muchas gracias."

Muñoz said: "Can you play it for us, Aviles?"

"Claro! Pero . . ." He looked up at the clock on the church steeple as the chimes struck midnight, then back to the chief. "The town is asleep. Perhaps if I play softly . . ."

"Play, Aviles! Play loud. Never do anything half-assed."

Muñoz and Jake sat on the steps of the presidencia; Bonifacio Aviles stood in the middle of the cobbled street. He raised the trumpet toward his mouth, then hesitated. He looked the instrument up and down and muttered:

"Qué milagro! Qué dia!"

And the chief smiled as the gardener pressed his lips to the trumpet as to a woman he loved.

Chapter

SEVENTEEN

It was late in the day, just after closing. The sun had set two hours earlier, and Homero was stacking the chairs on the tables of the Café Cristóbal Colón and sweeping up when a man came in with a bullfight poster and stood in the open doorway of the cafe.

He was a tall man of forty with a certain air about him, and he held the poster up to Homero as though he expected the provincial servant to gape in awe. It depicted a svelte banderillero in tight pink pants dancing away from a muscular black bull after having just embedded his two colorful darts in the bull's back.

But Homero doubted that the poster accurately reflected what would occur in the local arena. He had once been to a bullfight there but never returned to see the bulls taunted, tortured, and finally killed. The animals had seemed weak and indecisive—hardly like the one in the picture—and he felt for them.

"Can one put a poster in the window?" the man asked.

Homero leaned his broom against a table and approached. The waiter, the cook, and the owner, Don César, had all gone home, so Homero was now, theoretically, in charge. He studied the poster and pursed his lips.

"Qué es esto?" he asked, pointing to thick black type at the bottom of the poster. " 'Los forcados.' "

"You haven't seen them? Son fantásticos! They stand four in a line before a charging bull—without capes or swords or picas or any weapon whatsoever—and wrestle the animal to the ground with bare hands.

"Es bien loco."

The man shook his head. "No, they are the bravest of all." He looked Homero up and down. "In fact, you seem to me like a young man who might make a good forcado. There is a meeting of the local club tomorrow night at the school gymnasium."

Homero doubted, too, the man's contention that he might make a good bull-wrestler. Homero Gutiérrez was a skeptic.

For example, when the waiter at the Café Cristóbal Colón, Jesús Balderas, would whisper to the busboy about how the socialists would someday soon free Mexico from the clutches of the established families and the Revolutionary Party, Homero would nod agreement yet not believe a word. What Homero believed in was the power of Don Pablo Martínez, the local Revolutionary Party boss, who sat every day at his corner table in the cafe dispensing favors like candy. Still, to please Jesús, Homero once went to a socialist meeting and had his doubts confirmed. No one seemed to care at all about freeing Homero from his oppression; no one even talked to him, and he went home to his father's room without saying a word.

Nor did Homero trust the words of Marcos Celorio Villareal, the handsome gigolo who came into the Café Cristóbal Colón with gringas of all ages and who told Homero that he, too, could bed these women from Ottawa, Detroit, and Seattle who came to Mexico for sun and romance. All he need do was dance with them, tell them the lies they wanted to hear, and ask for it. It was that easy, Marcos would say, but Homero was skeptical. He had never before talked to a woman except for his mother and sisters and couldn't imagine saying something like that to one. Besides, he was fat. Not so fat as Don Pablo Martínez, but still heavier around the middle than a young man of twenty-one ought to be. But most twenty-one-year-old men did not work in a cafe where leftover pie, cake, and pan dulce were there for the taking. And most women would have nothing to do with a man who bused tables and swept the floor.

Thus he was also skeptical when the advance man for the traveling bullfight told Homero he might make a good forcado. For of all the things about which he was skeptical, Homero was most skeptical about himself.

"No, gracias. I am too busy with other interests," he said, thinking that one had to be very desperate for attention to do something so crazy.

Homero showed the man where he could tape the garish poster to the window, then finished his cleaning up.

Homero could hear his sisters' laughter in the dining room as he pushed through the front door of the house. He hung his jacket on a peg behind the door and followed the sound of their voices to the dining room, where he saw they had begun supper without him.

His mother sat at the head of the table with her infant grandson on her lap. Homero stood looking for a place to sit, but all the chairs were filled with his sisters and his cousins, and at times he wasn't sure which was which. The women all looked alike, talked alike, and were all his age, give or take five years, and none of them ever paid him any mind. As he stood by the table searching for a plate or a chair or a place to squeeze in, not one of them so much as glanced at him. Finally, he said, "Buenas noches," and his mother looked up as though surprised to see him standing there.

"Homero."

"Sí."

"What is it? What do you want?"

"Is there something to eat?"

His mother's eyes scanned the table, surveying empty platters and bowls. "I thought you would eat at the 'cafe.' "

Homero bit his bottom lip to keep it from trembling. She always said "café" as though it were a dirty word. Her two oldest sons had become professionals: one a travel agent in the capital, the other a schoolteacher in Morelia. But Homero had not done so well in school. He was too shy to mix with the others or to raise his hand in class. Since he was slow afoot, his teachers also thought him slow-witted; since he was too self-conscious to speak out in class, they thought he had nothing to say.

Homero now opened his mouth to speak, but under his mother's gaze words did not come. From his left he heard the voice of his sister Griselda:

"No, mother, he did not eat *at* the cafe, he *ate* the cafe."

They all laughed at this supposed witticism: his sisters, his cousins, his mother—even the ignorant child on her lap.

"It won't hurt Homero to miss a meal."

"For once."

He stood there for a moment looking at them all, then turned away and walked to the kitchen. Homero heard the laughter following him. They sounded just like the girls at school had.

In the kitchen he found some bread and cheese but no beer and carried his plate to his room under the stairs at the back of the patio. It was the same walk his father had made every night as long as Homero had known him.

In his room Homero kicked off his shoes and turned on the small black-and-white TV he had saved for. He sat on his narrow bed with legs crossed and the plate of cheese resting in his lap. The picture finally came into focus, and he saw that it was a concert of some sort. The television camera panned across the audience, where teenage girls—lovely, dark-haired Latinas—screamed toward the stage. Another camera now showed the performers. A young man in tight white pants—the vocalist—gyrated lewdly in front of an orchestra; on either side of him a woman in a skimpy costume with sequined crucifix stitched between her breasts danced frantically.

Homero wondered what the hell kind of concert it was—the audio on the set had ceased a week after he bought it. He had hoped for a football match tonight, or a baseball game. But it was the only channel that reached his pueblito.

He studied the buttocks of the dancers, who had now pivoted to display their comely backsides to the audience and the cameras, then looked down at the slices of dry cheese in his lap. He knew he shouldn't eat cheese that late at night; it always brought bizarre dreams. But it was all he had.

He dreamt first of the dancers, who had come to his room for a private performance, and it was very exciting before it

started going bad. They danced for him silently, pressing themselves against him. But then one of the women took the sequined crucifix from the front of her costume and began to
beat him with it. Then he was alone in the dark of his room,
hearing the crickets outside his door in the patio.

However, Homero soon again fell asleep and now stood
naked at the center of the Plaza de Toros with neither sword nor
cape. He heard laughter and looked up to the benches of the
arena. There townsfolk pointed at him standing nude on the
earthen arena floor and roared with delight. He felt something
behind him and turned. The bullfight advance man held up to
Homero a poster of a charging bull. The black animal leapt off
the poster and came at him, and Homero ran. He circled the
arena trying to escape but was too fat to scale the barrera. When
he finally managed to gain a grip at the top of the boards, his
mother came laughing from the crowd and pried his fingers
from the wall.

The great black bull still menaced him from behind, its
breath warm on Homero's back, and there was nowhere to go.
So Homero turned to face the animal, knowing he was about
to die. The bull came rushing toward him, and in its eye he saw
his sisters and his cousins and his father's corpse. The beast also
contained the waiter Jesús, the gigolo Marcos, and the other
men who lied to him, as well as his teachers and his school-
mates, who had taunted him and called him fatso. And suddenly he saw that he, Homero Gutiérrez, was the sacrificial
animal and the throngs who forever humiliated him the toreros
who sought his death. For an instant he stood transfixed by the
revelation, naked, angry, and alone. Then he kicked at the earth
and charged.

The next day seemed endless to Homero. He had not slept well and did not laugh when Jesús joked with him. He realized how much time Don Pablo Martínez spent at his table in the Café Cristóbal Colón and counted how many pieces of nut pie the overweight politico consumed during the day. The gigolo Marcos came in at ten a.m. to order a beer, and when Homero took the empty bottle away he noticed gray hairs behind Marcos's right ear.

Near closing time a middle-aged gringo couple came in and sat down while Jesús was in the kitchen. Homero looked anxiously to the clock above the crucifix on the wall and moved quickly to them, pulling the tablecloth from before them and saying, "Cerrado, terminado, no eat." They got up and left without a word, and Jesús never saw them.

At nine o'clock Jesús looked at the empty restaurant and slapped Homero on the back.

"I'm leaving, son. I have a young wife to tend to."

Within ten minutes Homero had the chairs stacked, the floor mopped, and was locking the door behind him.

As he passed through the zócalo, the fragrance of cilantro came to him from the cauldrons of the campesinas who cooked for travelers under the portales. But tonight the aroma did not make him think of food; it did not register in his brain or affect him whatsoever. He had but one vision in his mind, driving him forward like an angry bull.

At the school he saw light coming through the open gymnasium doors and stepped to them. Inside, four men in stockinged feet stood on thick tumbling mats that had been spread on the floor. Three formed a line facing the fourth, who came at them behind a wheelbarrow with a set of horns fixed to the front, and Homero's skepticism about becoming a forcado abruptly returned. Homero knew his life was sorry—some might even say pathetic—but this was worse. He had started to back out of the doorway when they spied him.

The man with the wheelbarrow immediately set it down and came to Homero, almost running.

"Ven, ven. Come join us. We are just beginning."

Homero did not move until the man shook his hand and pulled him toward the others.

The others, Homero now saw, were even sorrier than he. The thin man with long hair had but one eye, and when they shook hands, Homero noticed an obscene tattoo on his arm. Another, a blond gringo of Homero's age, wore a coleta, the torero's pigtail, and spoke little Spanish. His eyes were glassed and his pupils dilated. The third, Paco, a deaf-mute, was nearly as fat as Homero. Here at least, Homero thought, I will not be called the Silent One. The commandant of the wheelbarrow, Manuel, seemed pleased—no, relieved—to have a fourth forcado show up.

"We are proud to have you as a comrade, Homero Gutiérrez, and honor your courage. In the fiesta of bravery, the forcados are the bravest."

Homero soon saw that he was to be the bravest of the brave. Manuel put him, the largest, at the front of the line facing the wheelbarrow.

"Now we must move as one, as fish in the sea. As individuals we cannot subdue the evil of the bull, but together we mass the strength to vanquish him."

Nosotros, nosotros, nosotros—we, we, we—Homero said to himself. Yet this cabrón with the wheelbarrow will be safely behind the barricade.

"Now, Homero, we must remember two things. Both are vital. We must lay our chest squarely between the horns—not a thumb to the left nor to the right. And we must be moving forward. Your weight and that of your comrades must be advancing. Entiendes?"

"Es fácil."

"Bueno. Now let us try it once."

The deaf-mute Paco lined up behind Homero; behind him, the one-eyed man; and finally the gringo. Manuel took the wheelbarrow to the far end of the mat and came running. When the wheelbarrow was ten feet away, Homero charged, and the men behind him moved forward lockstep. He threw his chest against the horns and drove his legs. Homero felt the weight of the others on his back and heard a hollow grunt coming from somewhere deep inside Paco. The wheelbarrow halted and sledded backward, knocking Manuel to his ass. When all had stopped, Manuel looked up between the handles.

"Bueno!"

"It's easy," said Homero. There really was nothing to it.

El Club de Forcados del Bajío practiced for half an hour more. Then Manuel, using a piece of string and a ruler, took all their measurements and gave them each a stack of posters announcing the coming bullfight.

On the walk home Homero could not keep his eyes from the romanticized painting of the slender banderillero planting his banderillas in the shoulder of the snorting bull. But Homero did not see it as merely an idealized depiction of bravery. He saw himself.

When Homero arrived home from work Friday night, he closed the front door behind him, hung his jacket on the peg behind the door, and saw a package with his name on it sitting atop the old piano that was now used solely as a table. He picked up the package, the brown paper crackling as he squeezed it.

Then he noticed that a corner had been torn, as if someone had deliberately done so to look inside. He also noticed that the house was quiet, without the usual chatter and laughter of the women coming from the supper table.

He tucked the package tight under his arm and moved down the hallway that ran past the dining room and kitchen and opened onto the patio. But when he drew even with the dining room, he heard his mother's voice:

"Homero!"

He stopped and turned. They were all seated in silence around the dining room table: mother, sisters, cousins. All looked to him closed-mouthed.

"Sí?"

"Ven acá. I wish to talk with you."

Homero moved into the dining room and faced his mother.

"Tell me, Homero, what is in that package?"

"You should know. You tore it open to look inside."

Gasps came from the young women about the table. Homero felt his ears turning red and prayed that he could hold back his tears. His mother shook her head.

"Como tu padre. Without the common decencies. I suppose it is too late to do anything about that, but as long as you live under my roof, you will obey me. Now tell me what was delivered to you today in that package."

Homero felt his heart beating fast, felt his breath quicken in his chest.

"A uniform."

"De qué?"

"El Club de Forcados del Bajío."

A momentary silence hung over the table, broken then by his oldest sister, Griselda, who leaned over the table toward Homero and said:

"De forcados? The fools who jump on the horns of bulls and kill themselves?"

A chorus of screams and laughter filled the room, and Homero's mother threw her arms up into the air.

"Your father had no sense either. But at least he had the excuse of being drunk when he got himself killed."

Homero had not thought of that similarity: His father had been run over by a truck. Griselda said:

"Do not worry, Mama. With Homero, the bull will just bounce off."

Homero turned away from the laughter and crossed the dark patio to his room.

Once inside, he bolted the door, pulled off the white shirt and black slacks that were his busboy's uniform, and unfolded the uniform from the package. He laid it out on his narrow bed: beige kneesocks, brown torero pants, and a red-and-beige striped shirt. That should get his attention, Homero thought. He pulled off his black socks and began to dress as a forcado.

Homero stood in his uniform before the mirror on the bathroom door. He looked at himself there, then to the poster of the willowy banderillero that he held in his right hand at arm's length. Lying on the bed the uniform had appeared slim and elegant; on him he saw that it looked cheap and lumpy.

He stared again at the poster, but this time his eyes fell not on the dancing banderillero but on the charging black bull. The dream came back to him, the dream of the angry bull breathing on his neck while he, Homero, fled in fear. Now he saw he had misinterpreted his dream.

As a forcado, he would not threaten and impress those who had demeaned and humiliated him. Rather, he would bolt and run and show what a true coward he was. Homero saw that his mother was right: She had borne a fool.

Saturday morning Jesús noticed that something troubled Homero. The busboy dropped a plate on the floor, poured coffee on the tablecloth, and stood staring for long moments at the bullfight poster in the window.

"Qué pasa, joven? You look like you have seen a ghost."

Homero shot the waiter a glance that Jesús could describe only as fearful. The busboy's bottom lip even trembled.

Then, as the dinner customers were leaving for the bullfight, Homero removed his white apron and said to Jesús:

"I must leave for an hour. Or two. If Don César comes in, tell him I . . . I had to see the doctor."

"Are you sick, Homero?"

He shook his head.

"Then where are you going?"

"A la corrida."

"De veras? To the bullfights? I did not know you were an aficionado."

"I am not."

"Then what?"

Homero could not lie like the others. He looked at Jesús, then at his own shoes.

"Soy forcado."

Jesús stared at him as though trying to determine if Homero was playing a joke. Then he grabbed the busboy by the shoulders.

"Is it true? You are going to defy the bull bare-handed?"

Homero shrugged. "Sí."

Jesús put his arm around Homero's shoulder and called across the restaurant to Don Pablo Martínez, who sat finishing his dessert:

"Mira! Don Pablo! Es forcado. Homero Gutiérrez. He goes now to face death."

Don Pablo looked up and spread his hands as the cook and dishwasher came running from the kitchen. "Fantástico!" The politician raised his tequila glass toward Homero. "Here's to your courage, Gutiérrez, the bravest of the brave. Please drink with me. Jesús, tequila for everyone!"

Jesús poured shots for the help and for the few customers who remained. All stood and hoisted their glasses.

"Bravo, Homero Gutiérrez!"

They threw back the tequila, all except Homero, who stood staring at his shot glass. Don Pablo asked:

"Why aren't you drinking?"

Homero smiled a quivering grin that affected but half his face, then raised the tequila to his lips. He did not wish to tell Don Pablo that he hesitated to drink for fear of later wetting his pants.

Don Pablo insisted that they close the Café Cristóbal Colón for the afternoon so he might take the help to watch their colleague subdue the bull, promising to square it later with Don César.

Jesús fashioned a hand-lettered sign for the restaurant door:

CLOSED IN HONOR OF HOMERO GUTIÉRREZ, FORCADO

It reminded Homero of the notices put on shops when there was a death in the family.

They also all insisted that Homero change into his uniform of El Club de Forcados del Bajío at the restaurant, so they might escort him thus attired the two blocks up the hill to the Plaza de Toros amid the aficionados now streaming to the arena.

As they walked, Homero heard voices in the crowd:

"Híjole! Es Homero Gutiérrez!"

"Mira. The busboy will now clear the table for the bull."

"He is bigger than the bull."

Manuel and the other three forcados were waiting under the grandstand. Manuel seemed even more relieved to see Homero than the first time and handed him a long, red-and-white stocking cap, which, to Homero, resembled a dunce hat.

"It is traditional for the first forcado. Do not don it until you are at the center of the arena. Then turn to show it to the entire crowd and place it on your head with great ceremony. Do you have any questions, Homero?

"Sí. Where is the bathroom?"

Homero, Manuel, the deaf-mute Paco, the one-eyed one, and the gringo moved to watch the first corrida from the callejón, the narrow alley between the wooden barrera and the grandstand.

The cuadrilla with their capes went one by one from the callejón through the shielded burladeros into the ring to work the bull and study how it moved. Then came the picador on his padded horse to draw the first blood with his lance, followed by the banderilleros, who skillfully implanted two pairs of darts in the bull's shoulder. The angry bull chased the second banderillero toward the burladero where Homero stood, crashing into the planks just in front of him, and Homero leapt back.

It was not like the bull on the poster. It was bigger. And it did not sit still like the romanticized bull but charged faster than any man could run and took great splinters out of the barricade with its horns. Homero looked to his left and saw Manuel and his fellow forcados staring at him with concern.

At the eventual kill, Homero stood mesmerized. The torero deftly looped the curved espada over the horns of the charging bull and between its shoulders to its heart. The bull stopped and stood still for an instant, the silver sword handle gleaming against its black hide. Then blood gushed from its mouth and its nose, and the animal collapsed in the dust. The puntillero came with his dagger and pierced the top of the bull's head. The bull jerked once and died. The puntillero then used the dagger to slice off the bull's ear, which he handed to the matador, who paraded it around the arena.

They came with chains and white mules to drag the carcass away. A young man with a rake mixed the remaining blood into the dust, and Homero felt a burning in his chest, as if he might be sick.

He did not watch the spectacle of the second bull. Instead, Homero studied the people in the grandstand. He recognized aficionados with whom he had been at school; he saw his sister Griselda with her husband. In the front row sat Doctor Lourdes with his instrument bag on the bench between him and his nurse. When Jesús and the others from the Café Cristóbal Colón saw Homero, they waved and applauded.

After the second bull had fallen, the band at the top of the arena began another march, and Manuel said:

"Ahorita."

When the victorious matador had finished his promenade and the band broke into "La Virgen de la Macarena," Manuel said:

"Okay. Now. Buena suerte, y vayan con Dios."

Homero crossed himself, as did Paco and the one-eyed man. The gringo, whose eyes were still glassy, cracked his knuckles.

Homero sidled through the burladero and led them into the center of the arena amid the music and applause and cheers. He heard Jesús call, "Viva Homero!" and he wished that might hold true.

His stomach felt full of bees, and his legs wobbled as he walked. He tried to recall the state of mind that caused him to risk his life so readily and stupidly. He could not. Now Homero wanted more than anything else to be home, alone in his room, to remain the Homero he had always been. He felt as if he walked to the edge of the world. He went where there was no map and did not know what he would do there or who he would be when he returned—if he survived.

He reached the center of the arena and held the stocking cap high. He turned to all four points of the compass, and the crowd stood and applauded. But he noticed that the response was somewhat restrained, as if those in the bleachers somberly applauded their own good fortune for being in the grandstand instead of the center of the arena.

Homero placed the red-and-white cap on his head and turned to the door marked "Toriles," where the bull would enter. The Gate of Fright, he heard one of the cuadrilla call it.

The door swung open, and a dark brown bull with white horns came running down the ramp and into the dusty arena, and the crowd cheered louder. The bull circled the arena, ignoring the four men at its center, who turned as a phalanx to continually face the animal. Finally the bull saw them and stopped. It turned and eyed Homero and the stocking cap, thirty yards distant.

Homero stood rigid. He felt as if all his blood and all his being were draining into the ground. He stood petrified before the animal, feeling Paco's hands pushing on his back and hearing the words of the one-eyed man: "Vámonos, cabrón!"

But Homero could not move. Everything in the arena seemed to stop. A silence dropped over the crowd, and there was no noise in Homero's ears except that of his own blood pulsing through him. Then a whistle came down to them from the grandstand, and another. Someone yelled:

"Go to it, fatso."

Another cried, "Let's see what you are made of, Homero."

"Pan dulce!" came the answer from the other side of the arena, and the crowd laughed.

The men behind Homero pushed him forward.

"Do as you were told."

The laughter filled Homero's ears and his head; he felt them pushing from behind and heard their commands to advance. He saw his sister in the stands, hiding her face in her hands, and Homero felt tears coming to his eyes. He turned on the deaf-mute and screamed, "Stop pushing," pulling the cap from his head and swinging it at him. As he did, he saw the three other forcados gasp as one, and turned back. The bull was charging.

Homero flung the cap in the bull's direction and called:

"Pinche toro! No good son of a whore!"

The crowd heard him and cheered.

"That's it, Homero. Much anger! Olé!"

"Bravo, Homero! Go get him, muchacho."

But as the bull neared, snorting and pounding the earth with its hard hooves, Homero's first instinct was to run, and the one step he took backward was crucial. The bull caught him in the stomach and plowed him over, lowering its horns and driving Homero across the earthen arena floor.

The others ran to the barrera as the cuadrilla came racing toward the bull with their capes. Homero curled beneath the brown beast with arms wrapped around his head, tasting the bitter earth, wondering what was taking them so long. As the bull bolted forward to attack one of the pink capes, its hoof caught Homero square between the eyes. He heard a crack, and blood gushed from his nose and mouth as from a vanquished bull, spilling into the dirt.

Then the bull was gone, and someone was pulling Homero to his feet and running with him to the burladero. Once safely in the callejón, Homero looked down to his new uniform and saw that blood and mud covered the front of it and that his beige socks had been torn. When he looked up, the one-eyed forcado stood staring at him with his mouth open.

"You have no nose."

Doctor Lourdes came from the stands with his valise and his nurse. He studied Homero's face and said:

"The bull has given you a snout like his. We will take you to the clinic."

But Homero acted as though he did not hear what the doctor said. For still ringing in his ears were the momentary cheers of the crowd, the "Olés!" for Homero Gutiérrez, a sound he had never before heard. It lay so sweet on his ears and now in his breast that the pain he felt from the bull's hoof seemed but a small price to pay.

Doctor Lourdes had him by the arm and began to lead him down the callejón toward the passage beneath the grandstand. When Homero saw what he meant to do, he pulled his arm away.

"I am not finished!"

Lourdes shook his head. "Look at you, hombre. No one will blame you for quitting now."

Homero turned to Manuel and his comrade forcados, who all nodded agreement. The young nurse did so as well. Homero turned back to the doctor.

"Just stem the bleeding and let me continue."

Lourdes shrugged. "It's your face, amigo." And he nodded to the nurse to tend to Homero.

She took balls of cotton from the doctor's bag and fixed them in his nose. As she did, she whispered to him:

"He is right. You do not have to face the bull again if you doubt that you can defeat it. No one would fault you."

Homero leaned away and gazed at her. He saw a look of genuine concern on a face that was surely beautiful, more beautiful and sincere than any he had ever seen on a woman. He spoke softly yet firmly to her:

"Do I look like a man who would doubt himself?"

She studied his bloodied face for a moment, staring into his dark mestizo eyes as though attempting to divine his soul, and shook her head.

"No. You are most brave. Braver than all the matadors."

Homero felt his heart quicken and lighten as if to take wing, as if an espada he long carried there had been pulled from it. He turned to his comrades. "Vámonos, forcados!"

They moved as one out the burladero and into the center of the arena, and the crowd fell silent. The other representatives of El Club de Forcados del Bajío lined up behind Homero Gutiérrez, who faced the bull that had spilled his blood. He called to the animal:

"Estamos listos. We are ready. Ven, toro. Come do your worst."

The bull pawed the earth, then charged, and the four men moved as one to meet it, Homero laying his broad chest dead center between the tips of its horns. He felt the weight of his comrades behind him. Together they drove forward. The bull snorted, its legs buckled under their strength, and the dark animal collapsed to the ground.

Homero lay on the arena floor face to face with the defeated bull, the roar of the crowd enveloping him, the calls of "Olé, Homero Gutiérrez!" dusting him from above like powdered sugar. He stared into the bull's eye as though gazing into its brain and into its heart, and in the blackness there saw a wondrous vision, a universe of whole worlds he had never known to exist.

Chapter

EIGHTEEN

Jake Harting stood on the terrace of his room looking down to the patio below, where the gardener, Bonifacio, hacked away at the stump of the fallen jacaranda tree with an ax. Señora Pola appeared below, leaning on her cane, and called up:

"¡Jaque! Tienes un visitante. ¡El jefe!"

She made a flicking motion with her hand that in the States meant "Go away" but in Mexico meant "Come here." Jake signaled back that he would be right down and went inside his room to fetch a shirt.

El jefe. Chief of Police Muñoz, she meant. Jake knew he was straight with the law and wondered what Muñoz wanted.

As Jake came down the flight of concrete stairs from the terrace, Muñoz was saying to Bonifacio:

"Más abajo. Aquí. Then you will only have to cut once."

The gardener nodded, and Muñoz patted him on the back.

Jake shook hands with the chief and lifted his chin toward two chairs in the shade against the back wall of the patio. On the way Muñoz stopped to sniff an azucena, then removed his police cap and, with a sigh, lowered himself into a chair. Jake sat next to him and noticed that the chief's hair and mustache were almost coal black despite his age, which Jake put at fifty-plus.

Muñoz gestured at Bonifacio working in the sun.

"It is good to sit in the shade and watch a man work."

Muñoz spoke to Jake in English. He spoke it pretty well, and it was better than Jake's Spanish. Jake said:

"Bonifacio is a hard worker. In the States now we have machines to do the hard labor—or Mexicans. Americans no longer lift garbage cans or pick apples: machines and Mexicans."

Muñoz smiled and studied the gardener.

"We work hard, if not often smart. My family, too. I was born in Texas while they were picking."

Señora Pola appeared on the far side of the patio carrying a tray, moving toward the men sitting in the shade. She balanced the tray in one hand, leaning on her cane with the other. Jake rose and went to take the tray from her, which held two tall glasses of milky liquid. Muñoz also rose as she approached.

"Siéntense, señores. Something for the thirst," she said and nodded toward the glasses.

The men each took a glass and drank.

"Pulque and pineapple—both very fresh."

"Gracias. Muy sabrosa."

She ambled away, and the two men again sat.

"Any more trouble with Bonifacio?"

Jake shook his head as he drank. "No. Sober and steady. I think the time in jail was a good lesson."

"I am not so sure. Without the trumpet, I am afraid, he

would again become murderous." Muñoz turned and put a hand on Jake's shoulder. "That is why I am here today. I had doubted your word when you promised to buy the trumpet. And when you brought it, I vowed to buy you a drink."

"Gracias. I'd like that."

"Plus we can celebrate the holiday."

"What holiday?"

"Híjole! I am a better American than you, and I'm but a half-assed American. Turkey Day, hombre! Thanksgiving! Where have you been?"

Jake looked at Muñoz and shook his head. "I've gone south."

Muñoz pulled the police car to the curb in front of the Legión Americana.

"The legion's the only place in town to get a traditional Thanksgiving dinner—except for the salsa verde instead of cran-berries."

They moved through a blue wooden door into a shaded patio set with folding metal tables and chairs. A dozen of the town's expatriate gringos sat at their Thanksgiving comida, while more were visible through the open door on the right, sitting at the bar.

Muñoz and Jake moved to a table shaded by a tall elm grow-ing from the center of the patio. A young woman came to them from the bar, smiling.

"Sus órdenes?"

Jake ordered a beer, and Muñoz did the same.

When she turned to leave, Jake saw her hand brush the chief's shoulder, and Muñoz's eyes followed her walk back into the bar. Muñoz saw Jake looking at him and shook his head.

"Ay de mí!"

"A pretty woman," Jake said.

"Smart, too. Smart and pretty is very dangerous."

"Yo entiendo."

"This one has started rumors that she is going to have my child. My wife believes the rumors, so I am sleeping on a cot at the presidencia."

"Can't you convince her otherwise?"

"That would be easier if the rumors were not true. Perhaps if I could find a husband for Altagracia and a father for the baby . . ."

"He could not be as smart as she is."

Altagracia returned with the beer and poured two glasses for the men. When she had gone, Muñoz raised his.

"To the New World. Viva Cristóbal Colón! Long live Christopher Columbus!"

They drank that beer and another, and Altagracia brought them their Thanksgiving meal.

"Do you wish to say a prayer?" asked Muñoz.

Jake shook his head. The men ate.

Muñoz chewed and said: "I have much to be thankful for— a mestizo born in the States, the best of both worlds: Mexican blood and an American passport. Of eighteen children, I am the only one."

Jake again raised his glass. "I salute your mother."

Swallowing, Muñoz held up two fingers. "My father had nine children with his first wife before she died. The second wife, my mother, was jealous of the first and demanded nine of her own. I am number eighteen."

"A lucky number."

"Claro."

Altagracia called from the doorway of the bar:

"Jefe! Teléfono."

"Quién?"

She turned away for a moment.

"Eduardo García."

"Tell him I am eating dinner and will call him when I finish."

Jake took another drink of beer, leaned back in his chair, and patted his stomach.

"This is very traditional. I've never eaten Thanksgiving dinner with an Indian—even a half-Indian. Or with beer. The Pilgrims' ale kept them alive the first winter. That and the Indians who taught them to hunt."

"Maybe they should have let them starve. Then I wouldn't have so many gringos to arrest."

Soon a young man in a police uniform came in through the door from the street, strode up to the table, and saluted.

"Jefe, hay un problema . . ."

"Siéntate, García. We are having a Thanksgiving dinner and require more Indians. Pull up a chair and have a beer."

"Pero . . ."

"Siéntate."

The young man sat, and he and Jake exchanged nods. Muñoz motioned to Altagracia to bring three more beers. García sat on the edge of his chair. Soon the waitress reappeared with three brown bottles and poured. Muñoz again raised his glass:

"To the Third World and life without rules." The three men drank, and Muñoz set down his glass.

"Okay, García. Now tell me your trouble."

"Pues, Sergeant Rosales was to drive me and my prisoner to the train station. But he has not returned from comida, and the train comes in fifteen minutes."

"Well, if you miss the train, take him on the bus."

"Pero . . ."

"But what?"

"It is better on the train."

"Why is it better on the train?"

García studied his socks. "No sé. I have never been on a train."

Muñoz turned to Jake and said in English:

"This is my life: patrolmen who interrupt my fiesta because they want to ride the train."

"Well, hell," said Jake. "If a damn Indian wants to ride the damn train on Thanksgiving, I think he should."

Muñoz looked at Jake for a moment.

"You are right, amigo. It is the least we can do. Altagracia! Six more beers—to go."

Muñoz circled the block and headed the police car toward the presidencia to retrieve the prisoner. As they passed the Calle de Correo, García called from the backseat:

"Mira! El coche del Sargento Rosales."

Muñoz stomped on the brakes, and the tires squawked to a stop. He jammed the floor-mounted shift lever into reverse, and the car whined backwards. Again he stepped on the brakes and sat with the engine idling, staring down the Calle de Correo.

"By the blood of Christ, I am slipping, Harting. I must be getting old."

Jake, too, looked down the street and saw a police car parked outside a house sealed behind tall metal gates topped with ornate wrought-iron designs.

"What is it?"

"That bastard Rosales has beat me to the punch with the dentist's wife. And her husband has been in jail two weeks already for killing her last lover. I am certainly slipping."

At the presidencia García ran inside and in a few minutes came out with a heavyset man handcuffed to his wrist. He pushed him into the back seat of the police car ahead of him, and they were off.

The train station lay two miles out of town down a largely unpaved road, which Muñoz drove at highway speed, a balloon of dust billowing from the rear of the car. The chief reached down for one of the beers Altagracia had brought them as they left the Legión, and handed it over the seat back to the prisoner.

"Here, Gordito. It may be a while before you have another."

"Gracias." He took the bottle from Muñoz and pried off the cap with his teeth.

Jake asked Muñoz in English where the prisoner was going.

"To Guerrero State. He robbed a bank there and shot a guard two years ago. But he has lived quietly in my town ever since."

Jake glanced at the short, fat man in the backseat enjoying his beer.

The car bounded over the dirt road. Muñoz sounded the horn at a brace of piglets that had wandered into the road, and they ran squealing as the car raced past.

The vehicle climbed a rise then nosed down, and the men saw the train sitting at the platform. But as the car slid to a stop in the dust beside the tracks, there came a series of clunking sounds, and the train began to move.

Muñoz flung open the car door and stood with one foot on the ground, waving at the locomotive. But it continued to creep away from the dilapidated station.

García meanwhile had El Gordito out of the car and stood silently watching the last coach disappear around a brown hill.

"It is never before on time," said Muñoz.

He spied a young man wrestling with a crate on the platform and called to him:

"Joven! Where is the next stop?"

He looked up and pointed down the track.

"Pantano."

"Gracias. García, get him back in the car."

Muñoz spun the car around in the dust and headed it back out the unpaved road toward town.

He drove now at nearly twice the speed as before, and Jake could see the 120-kph mark on the speedometer but could not see the needle. Muñoz said:

"Open me a beer, hombre. All this dust . . ."

Jake opened two beers, handed one to the chief, and looked at García, who shook his head. El Gordito said, "Otra, por favor," and Jake opened a third.

At the main highway Muñoz turned right and followed the twisting two-lane road through low hills of sand and rock. The road dropped and straightened momentarily. Across a field of scrub on their right they could see the tracks, but no train.

The road rose again and turned and dove to flatten out, and García said:

"Allí está!"

The train sped ahead, barely visible on the horizon. The road moved closer to the tracks and soon ran alongside them.

The police car gained ground fast, and after a few minutes they were pulling even. As they passed a sign that read "Pantano," they could see the town ahead and the highway crossing the tracks. Muñoz moved the car past the locomotive and looked out the window beyond Jake to the train.

"The bastard is speeding up."

Muñoz put his weight on the accelerator and leaned back in the seat as if he expected the car to take off.

"Vamos a chingar a este cabrón," Muñoz said, "or we will die trying."

Jake saw the engineer leaning out the window watching the police car, then looking ahead to the crossing. He sounded the horn on the locomotive. García muttered a prayer and crossed himself. The prisoner bent down to watch the train, beer bottle at his lips.

Muñoz put more light between the car and the locomotive, and the engineer lay on his horn. Ahead, the road rose and crossed the tracks where an **X**-shaped sign read, "Cuidado Con El Tren." The car flew over the tracks, and out his window Jake read the numbers on the front of the locomotive.

The police car landed hard, its undercarriage scraping the road. Muñoz glanced in the rearview mirror where both García and El Gordito were holding their heads.

Jake said, "Well done, matador," and the chief nodded once and spread his hands.

There was a cantina across from the Pantano train station, and after they put García and his prisoner on the train, Jake and Muñoz headed for it.

The late afternoon sun had dropped low enough in the sky to shoot a beam above the swinging front doors to the back wall. Jake and Muñoz moved to the end of the bar closest to the door, away from a party of five men in the back of the unlit cantina—the only other customers, with blackened hands and grease-smudged clothes. One of them threw back his head to let out a high-pitched yell. Another began to sing "La Paloma Blanca," and the others joined in.

The bartender came over. Muñoz looked at Jake and said: "I need a tequila."

"Dos tequilas. Añejos," Jake said.

The bartender broke the seal on a bottle of Oredain, poured two tall shots, and left the bottle on the bar along with a plate of split limes. They clinked glasses together, threw back the liquor, and poured more. Jake offered Muñoz a cigarette, and they both lit up.

The mechanic who had been yelling spied the two men at the bar and sauntered over with his beer. He spit at a bucket by the foot rail and missed, then fixed reddened eyes on the bottle of tequila.

"Oye, hombre, sweeten this for me," he said to Jake, holding out his red Tecate can.

Jake took the bottle from the bar and poured two ounces into the man's beer.

"Gracias. Gracias, amigo," he said, then stepped back and looked Jake up and down as though now seeing him for the first time.

"De donde eres?"

"El norte," said Jake.

"Usa? Los Estados Unidos?"

Jake nodded, and the man turned toward his friends.

"Miren, hombres! Un gringo."

His friends kept singing. He turned back to Jake.

"If you are a gringo, then buy me a drink to prove it."

"If one is able to recall," said Jake, "I have just done so."

The man stared down over his grease-smeared overalls to his beer can then again looked up.

"I do not remember this. It did not happen."

Jake shrugged.

The drunk said: "If you had bought me a drink, I would have known. Why are you lying to me?"

His compadres sensed that the conversation at the bar had

turned more interesting, and one of them began to drift in that general direction. Jake looked to the chief. Muñoz lifted his chin at the man with the beer can and said:

"Oye, hombre. That thou would permit us a private conversation."

The drunk focused now on Muñoz, scrutinizing his uniform. "And who in the name of Christ the King are you?"

"Yo soy el ley. I am the law. And I ask you not to molest my prisoner, for he is a dangerous man."

Jake looked at Muñoz and said in English:

"Thank you. Now he'll want me to kick his ass to prove that I'm dangerous. Thank you."

"Qué dice?" asked the drunk.

"He says that you are one sorry son of a bitch."

"Mande?"

The second mechanic arrived and was told by the first:

"The gringo travels to the penitentiary, and the general asks us not to fuck with his prisoner."

Now he, too, looked Jake up and down, and said:

"But we must fuck his prisoner to prepare him for the other prisoners."

The two men laughed, and Jake turned to Muñoz.

"This is getting ugly, Hector."

"Don't worry. I have marksmanship ribbons from the United States Army."

"Let's just leave."

Jake put forty pesos on the bar and grabbed the bottle of tequila. Muñoz snatched Jake's wrist and snapped a handcuff around it.

"These mestizos respect metal more than words," Muñoz said, and as he did the men backed away, staring at the shining esposas as though they were a sacred icon.

"This was a magical place for the Indians, Harting." Then he turned and gestured with his beer bottle at the thirty-foot-high concrete cross behind them. "For everyone."

Jake, leaning against the hood of the police car, looked out from the prospect to the shadowed valley below, took a pull from the tequila bottle, and chased it with a swallow of beer. He could see the lights of their town glimmering through the dusk on the far side of the valley, perhaps ten miles distant. Behind him a slice of orange sun was yet visible.

"Sí, muy mágico," said Jake. "But I don't think it is good magic."

Muñoz stood hands on hips, beer bottle in his left, his back to Jake. He turned, approached, and took the tequila bottle from the American.

"Tienes razón. Maybe the Aztecs made human sacrifices here. Or perhaps it was a place of punishment for the Spaniards. Or both. Even on warmest days one feels the cold in the stones."

Muñoz took a drink of tequila then drained off his beer. He hefted the beer bottle in his hand.

"Mira, joven. I will show you how I won medals in Vietnam and defended you from communism."

He threw the beer bottle high in the air, drew his revolver, and fired twice, the sound of the explosions cracking against the hard stones and echoing in the nothingness that surrounded them. The bottle dropped to the ground whole. Muñoz stared at it.

"There was a day when I could have opened a beer bottle at a hundred yards. I must be drunk. Just another drunken Indian."

Muñoz retrieved the tequila from where he had set it on the car hood, drank, and passed it to Jake.

"Beneath everything, we are Indian. The conquistadors demolished the Aztec temples, then built churches on the same sites with the temple stones. Beneath everything, we are Indian."

"It's different up north. The English started over. Blank slate."

"The English brought their women with them. The Spaniards did not. That is how my people began. I am part conquistador and part indigeno. Both conqueror and conquered."

"A rare combination: Indian and Pilgrim."

"Claro. We know both how to subdue and how to submit. Thus we will conquer the world. Look at California. Look at Texas. Trust me, Harting, before you grow old and die, the people in Minnesota will be speaking Spanish."

Muñoz pulled a fifty-peso note from his pants pocket and handed it to Jake.

"Mira. 'La Fusion de Dos Culturas.' I have seen this painting at Chapultepec. A conquistador in his suit of metal on his armored horse. He drives his lance through the stomach of a naked Indian, while at the same time the Indian plunges a spear into the Spaniard's heart."

"Is this before or after Thanksgiving dinner?"

"There is none in México. The Spaniards were not so hypocritical as the English."

"That's what Mexico lacks: a Thanksgiving dinner, where every mestizo invites both parts of himself to sit down and give thanks for being neither wholly conquistador nor wholly Indian."

"We do it every day, amigo."

Muñoz went to open the trunk of the police car and returned carrying a small automatic weapon with metal stock.

"I took this from a narcotraficante last month and have been wanting to try it."

He stood with feet spread and sent a spray of rounds toward the beer bottle lying on the sand. A cloud of dust arose there on the darkening plateau, and when it settled and the valley once again quieted, the beer bottle had disappeared.

It was dark by the time they returned to town. Muñoz steered the car to circle the zócalo, where the presidencia sat on the far side. Jake gazed out the side window and, under the portales on the west side of the square, saw a mariachi band in black costumes leaning against the wall.

"Mira. It's Bonifacio with his trumpet."

"That was a good thing you did, Jake, to buy him the instrument. He loves that piece of metal more than he loved his wife."

"The trumpet is new and shiny."

"Maybe that is the answer," said Muñoz.

He moved the car to the presidencia but did not stop. He circled the zócalo again and pulled the vehicle to the curb by the portales, where the mariachi band awaited a customer with a lover who required serenading.

When Bonifacio saw Jake and Chief Muñoz in the car, he came over with his trumpet and bent down to peer in the window.

"Buenas noches, señores."

Muñoz handed him the fifty-peso note and a twenty-dollar greenback.

"Bonifacio, do you know the woman at the American Legion, Altagracia González Reyes?"

"La mesera?"

"Sí. Take your band there and sing to her. But don't tell her who paid you. Entiendes?"

Bonifacio nodded.

"If she asks, tell her only that you and your band wished to honor her beauty."

The mariachis shouldered their instruments and moved off across the zócalo. Jake said:

"I did not know you were so romantic."

"I am Mexican, so I am very romantic. And because I am Mexican, I also believe in miracles. Perhaps Bonifacio and Altagracia will get together, and all our problems will be solved."

"Bonifacio y Altagracia. I feel as though I should genuflect."

"I would crawl on my knees to Mexico City should they marry."

"And if they don't?"

Muñoz shrugged. "Perhaps there is no resolution to my problem. But nothing is ever finished in Mexico: buildings, highways, marriage, love."

Jake reached his hand across, and Muñoz took it.

"Yo me voy," the American said. "All this talk of romance . . . I think I will go sleep with Marta tonight."

"Yes, Harting. Go to your woman. Go make a Mexican baby."

"I will try, Jefe. Y tu?"

Muñoz again shrugged.

"I will go to my little cot in the presidencia and sleep with my memories. And tomorrow, who knows? Maybe my luck will change. I have always been lucky."

Jake strode up the block toward Marta's casita, and Muñoz parked the police car in front of the presidencia. Sergeant Rosales was at his desk typing on a report form. When he saw Muñoz, he stood and saluted.

"Working late tonight, Rosales?"

"Sí. I had to take time off today to attend to personal business."

"Well, I hope you did not let down the department this afternoon."

Rosales opened his mouth as if to speak but said nothing. Muñoz moved down the hallway to his cot under the portrait of Pancho Villa.

He lay down in his uniform, hands behind his head, staring at the dark ceiling, visualizing there the conquistadors with their suits of metal, the Indians they slaughtered, and the Indian women they took to them.

As he sailed from consciousness into sleep, Muñoz found himself marching across an arid plateau. He heard footsteps behind him and turned. There he saw a line of mestizos marching in a cloud of dust, following him down a dirt road from a mountaintop. He noticed his mother and father directly behind him, and behind them his grandparents. The line of marching people stretched back miles and miles, curving up the mountain to its peak, where he saw a lone, armored conquistador astride a great horse, a beautiful, bronze Aztec maid in his arms.

Muñoz turned back to continue his march and now noticed his two wives, one on either side, and in front of him saw his children and their children and their children's children and all the children yet to be born, all marching, mestizos eighteen abreast, moving down a dusty road that led across a great valley and disappeared over the horizon into an orange sun.